VIOLETS

Alex Hyde

GRANTA

Granta Publications, 12 Addison Avenue, London W11 4QR

First published in Great Britain by Granta Books, 2022

A CIP catalogue record for this book is
available from the British Library.

1 3 5 7 9 10 8 6 4 2

ISBN 978 1 78378 727 2
eISBN 978 1 84708 729 6

Typeset in Quadraat by Patty Rennie
Printed and bound by CPI Group (UK) Ltd, Croydon, CR0 4YY

MIX
Paper from
responsible sources
FSC
www.fsc.org   FSC® C171272

For my father,
in memory of my
grandmother.

PART ONE

1

There was the enamel pail of blood. She couldn't think what she had done with it. She hated the thought of someone else emptying it.

Was that what it meant, lifeblood? Placental, uterine. She had seen the blood drop out of her into the pail. It came with the force of an ending.

And the pain. Her lower right side. The gush of the blood. Thinnish, not thick. Not like anything carrying life.

Violet opened her eyes.

She had been carried. Down the stairs.

Yes, Fred had been there.

She thought of her nightie, sopping wet. Someone had brought the motor car, must have borrowed it from Reg. She had been concerned about the blood but Fred had already thought about towels and blankets, that was good.

She was in a day-lit space. The large windows were criss-crossed with brown tape. Nurses passed and the floor shone under their shoes. The walls were thickly painted and white.

Bright.

Fred was there.

Violet, love?

He'd been holding her hand but now let go. He filled her field of vision, a thin smile on his lips. He looked tired.

You look tired.

Your mother's been round, he said. Everything was fine. At home, he meant.

Maybe her mother had emptied the pail. She must have moved it from the landing where Violet had crouched down. It must have clattered and slopped. All that blood.

She should have seen to it. She would have known. A dark reflection, a depth of loss.

Fred was talking about Reg and the Morris, and Father Lewis had dropped by.

He was meant to be on exercise, that was right.

Elizabeth had packed her some things, he said. He indicated the suitcase at his feet. Her sister would know what she'd need. A mirror, clean clothes, her bedjacket with the tie at the neck.

Had he collected their rations and told Mrs Oldman to save him some eggs?

Vi. You just need to rest.

He took her hand again in his. His hand was square, thick.

Violet? he said.

She thought that if she stared straight ahead, she could keep it all in.

Yes?

You know the baby's gone?

See?

See her, there?

Yes, you.

Pram Boy, pill-boy, you know who.

No flood for you,
no gush or release
of blood into water,
filaments and threads.
For it is you who will be carried
while the others are shed
(I'll take the one with the curls, your mother said).

~

Violet slept some more and when she awoke some of the others were up and about. She recognised it now, the same ward she'd been on before. Birmingham Women's Hospital. Nothing to do with the war.

It was later when the doctor came. Violet pushed herself up and tried not to wince. The pain was immense.

Just a few stitches, Mrs Hall.

He was clipped and matter-of-fact.

I've spoken to your husband. You were aware of the pregnancy, yes?

Violet nodded.

Ectopic, the doctor said.

An egg, fertilised, but attached to the wrong place. Growing all the same and for weeks.

About fourteen, we think. That's quite a stretch.

Violet cast her mind back. Missed periods, skipped beats.
October it was, Fred was on leave. And she could hardly
believe it had happened straight away. She was one week
late, then two, then three. Then time slowed right down.
Like cocking your head to catch a very faint sound.

And she'd watched the nights draw in, the trees lose their
leaves, thinking all the time about next July.

July 1945. A summer baby, bright blue skies.

There's one more thing.

The doctor coughed.

It seems that it was twins, Mrs Hall.

Violet felt the air hauled out of her lungs. She couldn't
take it in. There had been two of them, holding on.

Two children at once?

What a handful! she thought, until she remembered they
were gone.

Gone, Pram Boy, done for, through.

Not you though, Pram Boy, son of a Pole

Son of a soldier with his gun.

So let's just say
(for you will always get your way)
it's for the best.

Oh yes.

Coo-ee cuckoo, find your nest.

Had they held on to her, or she to them? It didn't matter, in that wrong place. The enamel pail, its dark blue rim, and the thin metal handle with the wooden grip. She might have rolled up her sleeves and plunged her hands right in. Searching in the rust-tinged liquid.

For twins.

The doctor was looking through her notes. Saying something about her history of cysts, the removal of her left ovary a couple of years ago.

Perhaps her mother had been in. She would have known what to do. Cold water, not hot. She would have got down on her hands and knees and tamped the stains with a cloth. Then she would have carried the pail downstairs and rested it on the mat while she unlocked the back door then poured it out.

Into the drain in the yard, with the suds and the silt and the dirt.

The foetuses had been surgically removed, the doctor said. Along with her womb.

Violet blinked. One of the other patients shuffled slowly past her bed.

And so.

There was a pause.

You'll understand that you will not be able to bear children, Mrs Hall?

He looked suddenly small, like an awkward schoolboy in his collar and tie.

Thank you, Doctor.

Violet smiled politely. The doctor nodded and moved on.

2

No. Still nothing.

Violet pulled up her knickers and swilled out the pan.

Every time she would check. Every slight feeling of wet. She would go to the lavatory or somewhere she could pull up her skirt, hoping for a bleed. But no, there was only the pale slick smeared on her inner thighs, the glistening string like egg white.

She shut the lid and sat down again, lit a cigarette.

She didn't feel like going back to the house, across the yard. Back to her mother sitting there chewing each mouthful too many times. Sitting there silent, watching for signs.

Signs of what? She couldn't have known.

Usually, they had their periods at the same time. Since Violet was about fourteen, just after her father died. They never said anything but they would know, taking bowls of water with bicarb of soda upstairs, the rags soaking under the beds, the water turning redder as they slept.

Violet sighed in the smoke that she had just exhaled. She stared at the back of the door. Torn-up squares of the *Rhondda Gazette* hung on a nail in the wood. News about farming and sport mixed up with the Western Front.

Best use for it, wiping your arse.

Violet stretched up her arms, rubbed her lower back. Her breasts had been sore, there was that. She was constipated, bloated. Though not in any way that showed.

No. Her mother couldn't possibly know.

Oh ho, Boyo!
But you are there,
pretty as a picture, coming down the stairs
Caught on a moon-edge, you came with the tide,
A boy all coy and evolving,
known only by what you are not.

Son of a bloodflow, stopped.

By the time Violet came in, her mother was clearing away.

I thought you'd finished, you took long enough.

Violet rinsed her hands, flicked the water off.

No, Mother. Here.

She took back her plate and ate the rest standing up.

She had always had an appetite. When her father was alive, he used to say that she had hollow legs. She was tall and lanky like him. Big feet, broad shoulders, flat chest.

Taller than her mother by the time she was ten.

Then he had died and her mother bought the shop. Then the war came and someone had suggested they take lodgers in. Wounded men, sent by the convalescent home, billeted with them for weeks, sometimes months.

Her mother's friends would all call in, coo and fuss, say it was good to have a man about the house again.

Until this last one. There'd been no one else since then.

No, because that was the end, Pram Boy,
where you began

Clinging on,
with your Papa seed, semen dried, long gone
on the train to Aberdeen.

For you saw your moment,
his seed barely spattered and his cock withdrawn,
forming like you'd found a place

to burrow down, laughing.

Now you're furiously filling up womb-space,
a keeping, a kept place
       Lurking like a bad joke,
like something about her no one can quite put their finger on
For now only an inkling
(your Papa's eye a-twinkling)
sometimes,
       a sick feeling.

Upstairs, Violet pulled the blackout curtains shut. She
threw her clothes onto the chair. She took her knickers
down, checked the crotch, twisted the seams so that the
stiff stain cracked and she picked a few bits off.

Her skin pimpled in the cold. Her sides were straight and
long, stomach flat as a board. Her nipples were darker
than before. She moved her hands across her breasts, felt
the slight weight of them drop.

She could hear her mother coming up. Violet listened
for her tread on the landing, the creak of the boards
underfoot. She would know that Violet was awake by
the strip of light under her door. They could have called
goodnight, but they never did.

Violet turned off the light.

She closed her eyes, counted the weeks in her head.

It was just before Christmas when the soldier left. She hadn't written to him yet. He'd given a little shrug when they said goodbye. To show that he couldn't help it, that he thought it was a shame.

Sorry I'll never see you again.

3

When the nurse came to change her dressings, Violet asked to have a look. The incision was low down, a puckered line about two inches long. It was oozy and puffed-up. You could see where the black thread had been knotted off.

She winced as the nurse swabbed.

They've made a pig's ear out of that!

It was meant to be a joke but the nurse was a bit off.

Still, most of the others were nice enough. When her sister Elizabeth came to visit she would watch them busy about. Liked their white uniforms, she said. Violet wondered at the rubbish that went through her head.

It was another few days before Fred could come again. He'd had to go back to his unit straight away.

We nearly lost you, Vi. That's what he said when she woke up.

No bad thing for the men to realise what they'd got, her mother said. But Fred wasn't really like that.

He was in uniform when he arrived. She saw the others stop and look. He wasn't tall but he carried himself well. He went to the desk, took off his cap. The matron was smiling at something he said.

Yes, everyone liked Fred. A bit of a laugh but never too much.

He brought her some toffees in a paper bag. Where he got these things she never asked.

They went for a walk around, better than everyone on the ward listening in. She moved slowly, holding on to Fred's arm. Their shoes squeaked on the lino floor. He was telling her about the jobs he would do at the house. He'd fix the porch roof, he said, ready for when she came out.

There was a pause.

Vi?

She knew there was something else, something more.

He'd had his orders to deploy.

Sod's law, he said, with a helpless look on his face.

But she remembered he was on the list for overseas? He thought they had agreed, he'd told her that he'd volunteered.

Then something splintered and broke and she said the words like she was spitting them out.

Sod's law, is it? Sod's law? For Christ's sake, Fred.

Because she was sick of it all. After France, and Africa before. That stupid bush hat he still wore for the summer when he came home. And the boy in the Gold Coast who fetched him water for his bath, the boy he taught to play draughts, who stole his cigarettes and Fred just laughed. And all their stories down the pub, all the souvenirs and photographs of men with their chests bare, shorts square with pulled-up socks and boots.

Sod's law.

They were quiet for a while, standing at the end of the corridor. Outside it was nearly dark. The wind whipped the rubbish from the bins across a scrappy bit of grass.

Fred tried to take her hand.

It was Burma, he said, and Violet asked him where on earth was that.

East of India, against the Japs. They were shipping people right away for decent pay and a jump in rank.

Come on, Vi. It won't be so bad. And things are a bit different, now.

Violet flashed him a look, quick as a dart.

Different how?

Now there won't be the baby, I mean.

No, Violet said. Now there won't be the twins.

4

The factory was on the outskirts of town. They bussed the women in from all over the valleys but Violet came on her pushbike. It was a fifteen-minute ride. The only other was a girl called Gwyn. She was untidy and slow. She would come loping up to the bicycle racks as Violet was untucking her trousers from her socks. They'd say hello but not much else.

The overalls they'd been given were the same as the men's. Some of the girls had cinched theirs in at the waist but Violet left hers loose. She liked to feel her body move beneath, where they were tight, where they were slack.

She sat down on a bench and watched the rest of them on their break. Clumps of men smoking, girls looking over their shoulders, laughing.

Not that it helped. The men still resented them coming in. Doing their jobs better than them.

They had half an hour for lunch. Violet pulled an apple from her satchel and took a bite. Its flesh came away in a hard, crisp flank. She flipped it into her mouth and spat out a pip. Then she took out a piece of paper and a pen.

She'd only got as far as the date and her address. Because what did she want? For the soldier to come down from his billet, propose marriage and take her away?

That'll be the day, Pram Boy, girls like her.
The trudging moor-girls,
poor girls,
war-working knocked-up shop girls.

He would ask if the baby was his. If she was sure. Which she was.

Which some weren't, of course.
Those that hid themselves away,
gave birth to babies
on cold floors
alone, groaning them out,
babies born carping for breath
flailing their limbs
and some of them, Pram Boy,
dark   brown   skinned.

It couldn't have been any of the others, Violet thought.

It couldn't have been Ted Barnes, when the room had smelled of mildew and coal dust trodden into the rug. The ceiling was stained with smoke. He had kissed her like a hole he could poke through, pawed at her blouse. She knew it would happen when he stood up and took off his boots, looking down, hopping about as if she might get away. Then the slap of his belt as he bent it back on itself.

It was easier with Len Shale. Under the bridge in the summer when the river was low. He pulled her knickers to the side. She didn't mind. He asked her afterwards if it was nice.

Nice.

Then he'd said, buttoning his trousers and straightening his cap, I'll leave you to mop up.

No, the soldier hadn't been like that.

No, Pram Boy, lucky you.
As the last slick of come came out of her later,
standing in the queue.

Call it an opportunity, Little Boy Blue.

She remembered when they first met. He was sitting at the sewing machine in the kitchen and she came in through the back.

There was something about the way he moved. Stiff round the middle with his wounds.

And the rattle when he pressed his foot to the treadle.

And the silence when he saw her, and stopped.

And they had been all in a rush. With what? With the flush, for him, of not being dead? Having shrapnel spinning through your middle and your organs miraculously untouched? Just a scar like a tear, still tender when he pressed his body against her in the woods. Still making him flinch even as he was rough, lifted her up, his fists full of her flesh, holding her thighs, butting her face to the side like a bull breathing into her neck.

Yes. Pushing, they pushed.

Fucked, Pram Boy, fucked.

It was the only thing that made her feel alive. When he pushed inside her, when she knew she was about to come.

And now?
You are sump oil and filings,
industrial waste,
Axel grease
smeared on your Mama's face.

The factory bell rang. Violet screwed up the piece of paper and stuffed it in her bag.

The chargehand was standing by the door watching them all file in. Violet had to turn sideways to squeeze past. He hocked back some phlegm and spat on the floor, kicked the wooden block from under the door and let it slam.

Violet took her place at the machine, tightened the chuck and lowered the drill bit into place. She thought of the soldier sitting at the sewing machine, his hair carefully parted on one side.

How, then, could this be a surprise?

No, that was the thing. Everything had its price.

The siren went and the power hummed on. Violet put her foot on the pedal and brought the drill down into the plate.

Then she did it again, and again, and again.

5

It had been two weeks, Violet was impatient to be discharged.

Fred had been moved to a barracks in Kent. They didn't waste their time. A week on exercise and he was shipping out, so he'd come to say goodbye.

She walked him out of the ward. They stood there in the glare of the electric lights. She brushed the shoulders of his tunic, straightened his tie.

Acting Sergeant. He'd already sewn on his stripes.

Violet smiled and patted his chest, rested her head beneath his chin. His hand was in her hair. Then he looked at his watch.

I'll be off then, love.

He said it as if he was popping to the yard.

They still hadn't really talked. About what happened, that there had been twins, that they were gone, that there would be no trying again. But Violet had the same dream every night. She would be carrying twins, one in each arm. It made sense. She had carried them. Only terribly, perishingly, in the wrong place.

The thought must have struck him then because Fred said he was sorry again. For going away? For everything else? She had no idea how he felt, he'd been so careful, so reserved.

My sympathies, he might have said.

And Violet thought, can an unborn child be dead?

Yes, Pram Boy, that's them.

Fallopian dwellers, they were scraped out
Twins caught just divided,
wrongly formed or mis-attached.
And she, perhaps, had something wrong, they said.
So the husband signed the form
and they took everything out instead.

When she got back to the ward, the bed next to Violet's was suddenly occupied. The woman was lying on her left side, asleep. She had dark hair and pale skin.

Irish, Violet thought. Pretty, but poor.

Her hand on the pillow was dry and cracked, her nails

chewed down, knuckles red raw. There was an exhaustion about her that persisted through sleep.

Violet sat on her bed, managed to swing her feet up despite the pain. She was bored. The ward was busy with new admissions but most of them were middle-aged. Violet watched them all trudge up and down, padding about in their dressing gowns.

She thought of her best friend Flo. It'd be lunchtime at the factory by now, they'd all be chatting and joking around. And Fred going off on the boat. Plenty of men from his unit had signed up.

So it was just her stuck here on this bloody ward. 'Women's troubles'. Typical.

The woman in the bed next to her tried to turn. Violet heard her cry out with pain. She struggled to sit up, frowned, gave Violet a confused nod.

Violet was right. Her voice was fast and soft with inhalations when she spoke.

Yes, she grew up in Ireland, she said.

Her and all the rest. Though Violet's mother came from Galway, of course. Married an Englishman, moved up in the world.

Violet offered the woman a sweet from a bag. They rolled them noisily around their mouths, chatted about the ward, what they were in there for.

The woman had eight children, she said, the eldest was twelve.

Oh!

She was talking more easily now, about how they had taken everything out, some problems down below. And she wasn't sure what would happen with her husband, she said.

Come again? Violet wasn't sure what she meant.

You know? *In the bedroom?*

Violet laughed out loud. But the doctor will tell you, it doesn't mean no more of *that*! Quite the opposite, in fact.

Later, when the doctor came, Violet asked.

My dear! he said. We may have taken the cot, but the play-pen is still there.

The woman looked warily at them both.

Violet smiled. She must remember that, the doctor's little joke.

6

Violet cycled the mile to the woods with the letter in her hand.

It had been a week since she wrote. No pleasantries, no jokes. She got straight to the point.

Pregnant. Eight weeks late.

She didn't ask the soldier what he wanted to do. After all, she wrote, this isn't happening to you.

No. It was her body that was swelling up like a balloon, damp with sweat, wet between her legs.

And here was his reply, postmarked Aberdeen.

She hadn't opened it yet.

In the woods it was wet and barely light. Possibly there was rain, possibly just mist. Wisps of hair stuck to her cheeks. She climbed the upper path along the stream. The envelope in her hand felt limp.

They'd come here a lot. They would walk up in silence, arms folded, heads down against the cold. Until there, in the woods, it forced them together, the slip and solidity of the mud, the tree roots tripping them up.

Down, down
where they trudged, Pram Boy
Wetly in the afternoons
or crisped the morning frost,
sometimes a little lost
for conversation but no matter,
soon their hands would feel
what they could not say,
warmed between thighs,
sighed upon, cupped and blown.

And my, how you've grown!
A boy all sewn of weed and wet,
leaf mould and animal spit;
spores they carried back on their clothes
that they brushed off,
done in a rush
And you?
You were caught on a branch
with twig-snap, bits of rot.

Something lodged.

Anyway.

They could not have known
that you had dropped in, like a stone
        Perhaps a faint splash that they heard but ignored,
quick to come.

Plink.

Begun.

Violet leaned against a tree. She was out of breath. She felt the empty flip of her stomach and retched. Then she spat, wiped her mouth and carried on up the pass.

It was usually on Sundays when they walked here, after lunch. In the kitchen while she grabbed her coat, her scarf, took gulps of tea, he would be watching from the doorway.

His slow smile, his creased eyes. His taking care over things that she rushed.

Like when he helped with the washing-up. She would wait while he hung up the cups and stayed each one with his hand, stacked the plates without making a sound. She would mock him and sigh, tap her watch, then he would scold her for remnants of food on a dish, come close by her side, slide it gently back into the sink.

Violet came to a clearing by some rocks, threw the letter down and took off her coat.

And it was there that they would pull at each other's clothes. Just enough to get in. Then the jutting of his chin, the noises he made as he pushed her hard against a tree. The sting of a graze and the wheeze of her breath knocked out of her chest; his wince of pain as he lifted her up, his fingers digging into her flesh.

Quick as it was, uncomfortable and brisk, they always laughed afterwards, felt lighter on the way back. As if they had won. Pulled one over on everyone.

You say sod? Sod them. Yes?

Damn and blast!

He taught her swear words in Polish then pretended to be shocked.

~

Violet felt cooler now. She sat down, opened the letter and held it in both hands.

There was a page of neat writing and another small packet, sealed. Inside the packet were two white pills. They rattled into the corner, dry as chalk. Violet guessed what they were for.

If she had prayed at all, she'd prayed for this. For something to make it come away, unstick.

She tipped them out. The pills sat brightly in the palm of her hand. She closed her fist, was tempted to roll them like dice, let someone else decide. Fate, chance, God?

He loves me, he loves me not.

Violet read the letter. He was sympathetic, polite. As far as the language would allow.

Sorry for the trouble you find.

It was more than she was likely to get from anyone else. The pills were from a doctor he knew. He was vague about what they would do, how exactly they worked.

Please check if really true.

As if it was a lie. As if he needed proof. Or a bleed, until whatever was in there was gone, out, falling in ragged clumps. Strings of congealed blood.

Violet stared at the page of cursive, his elegant hand. She had watched him write letters in English before. They would be sitting at the kitchen table and he would ask her the words for various things. The words were always gentle, domestic. Words like 'clock' and 'thread'.

Once she asked him if there was someone else, up there in Aberdeenshire. He shook his head.

The way he watched her as she quartered an apple, cut him some bread. All that hanging about in doorways, breathing the same air.

And just like that, with a flick of her wrist, Violet threw the pills into the stream.

They sank to the bottom, bright stars among the weeds.

There, take heart, Pram Boy, you see?
Yolk sac floating, placenta growing in
all smooth with your transparent skin
Greedy, fucked there
on the make;
a stone's throw, a pill-shake.
And those other mothers' wombs removed,
while you the perfect pill-boy settle in.

So feel her, Pram Boy, scrambling down
then pedal-press and pushing into town.
Late late late to the factory gate
see she coasts and weaves, riding off the saddle,
arms locked, deep
                    breaths into her chest,
watched by old women on doorsteps
and some men,
shoulders sharply shrugging them off.

Careful, Pram Boy, feel her push on,
leaning into the corner,

gone!

Because more than anything, Pram Boy, your Mama wants to run.

Or do you think she wants to fall?
Spoke herself, veer across the road,
a clatter of bones,
          a hip-crush
Black and yellow hues her skin.
Feel she slows to think if she can do it,
tests the front brake,
recalls the
          flip-throw toothbreak
of a dozen girlhood falls,
contemplates her fate, and yours.

No.

Of all the King's horses
and all the King's men,
No one would put her together again.

7

A few days after Fred left, Violet was discharged. Her father picked her up. He waited with his coat tucked under his arm, unsure where to look as Violet did the rounds.

They got on the number eight bus through town. The muscles of her stomach throbbed around her scar. She remembered lying curled up in the back of the car, her knees up to her chest.

When they got home her father carried her case upstairs, lit a fire, hung about until Violet offered him a cup of tea.

No thanks, pet. I'll leave you be.

When he had gone, she walked slowly into each room, touching the backs of chairs, straightening the table-cloth. The houses on their street were all the same – two up, two down. The front room had a fireplace tiled in green. The back was where they ate and where the wireless was. It led into the kitchen, then out into the yard.

Violet checked the pantry, everything lined up on the shelves. Then she walked slowly up the stairs, leaning heavily on the rail.

The landing was dark and she peered down at the rug, felt it with the back of her hand as if it might still be damp. She went into their bedroom at the front. The bed was freshly made up. Then she walked back across the landing and opened the other bedroom door.

She paused, caught by the smell of paint from when they'd decorated a month before. Now she saw it for what it was. A blank space, an empty box.

It was after New Year, when Fred had a few days off. Violet had worn one of his overalls and tied her hair up in a scarf. Hanging the paper, swiping great arcs of paint, they had told each other the names they liked.

And in her mind, she had filled it up, that room. She had imagined it full of life. Now she couldn't even go in. Her limbs wouldn't move her from the doorway into the newly painted white. Into the pale, low shafts of light that cut across.

The best light in the house. South-facing, warm and soft.

Where she might have laid them in their cot.

Two peas in a pod.

8

Violet got the eight o'clock train from Pontypridd to Cardiff. The recruiting centre was in a Methodist church hall. It had the air of a village fete. There were trestle tables and posters pinned on concertina boards. Military personnel hung about, some of them crossing to different stalls to chat.

The Army section was at the back. In a corner to the right a woman in uniform stood sternly in front of a sign.

Auxiliary Territorial Service, ATS.

The woman asked if Violet was there to join up.

Yes.

Yes, *Ma'am*. Good!

She took a form from a cardboard box and Violet gave her full name, age and address.

There would be a medical examination and a trade test. Spelling, arithmetic, basic things like that.

How long will it take, until I'm called up?

The sergeant gave her a look.

In a rush are we, ducky?

Violet felt her cheeks flush.

The woman went through the forms.

They're shipping out to Italy pretty quick. Naples. I'll put you down for that.

The hall was filling up, some men were milling about. Violet watched them walk nervously around, the officers looking them up and down. They seemed so young. They must have been waiting this whole time. Since '39, since they were twelve, thirteen.

Violet was moved on to a waiting room at the side. She flicked through the papers on her lap.

Private Davies, V. E.

Italy.

She knew the fighting there was bad. The only other thing that came to mind was Rome. St Peter's and the Pope.

After a while the medical orderly came. He led her to a small room with three chairs against the wall, then Violet heard her name called from behind another door.

The doctor looked up briefly from his desk and told her to undress.

Violet went behind the screen, felt her breath quicken and her nipples harden in the cold. She stood in her petticoat and the doctor indicated the scales, checked her measurements, noted them down. Then he moved around her body while Violet stared straight ahead.

Take three deep breaths.

The doctor pressed the stethoscope to her chest, then took her wrist between his fingers, looked at his watch, let it drop.

Finally, after she had read from charts and he had watched her walk in a line with her arms outstretched, he sat down again at his desk.

Violet stood there in the cold.

He asked about a history of this or that, any episodes or fits.

And menstruation? Your monthly periods?

Violet swallowed, felt her throat constrict.

Regular, Sir.

Good.

There was the dull thud of a rubber stamp and the doctor signed the forms, handed her a copy without looking up.

A1. Medically Fit.

That'll be all, Private. Dismissed.

PART TWO

9

Let me tell you how it was, Pram Boy, for you could not see.

There was a vessel beyond
your vessel
& beyond,
the sea.

The troopship SS *Duchess of Richmond* would have been somewhat grand in its day. They marched in through what felt like a drawbridge in its side but once you were in, you could see what it would have been like. Before the war. Before it was painted grey. In its transatlantic days.

Violet boarded with a couple of Wrens and two other women from the ATS.

Odds and sods, someone said.

The others were anxious to find their cabins, settle in. Violet went straight to the main deck.

The atrium was like a country house, emptied out. Carpet rolled up, rusty stains on the bulkhead walls. Wooden benches bolted down. On the upper level there were ornate pillars, some mirrors, though most of them were cracked.

Some larger units had started to board. Violet stood to the side as the hordes pushed through. The men moved like sheep butting into one another's backs, thick-headed, eager to touch. Any one of them she might have recognised from home. From the factory, from the foundry, from the bookies, from the farm. They all looked alike. Pale, darting eyes. Working men, short back and sides.

Violet felt hot, her tie was too tight. She found her way out to look over the dock.

More crowds of men surged forward in a block. She could hear the bang and roar of the chains loading supplies. Dockers passed cargo along in a line. In the midst of it all, a group of women stood. Their faces were upturned, some of them holding on to their hats. They seemed oddly stuck, jostled together as everyone else flowed past.

Violet lit a cigarette. The deck was getting crowded with men leaning over the rails. They were hooing and shouting and messing around. Someone pushed past.

Hey! Mind out.

The man swung round, did a double take, looked her up and down. A couple of the others grinned.

Violet sniffed, hitched her bag onto her back.

What's the matter, cat got your tongue?

The soldier looked unsure, his friends brayed. Violet walked away.

~

They had been issued with various meal chits and dockets along with an advance of two weeks' pay.

Violet patted her pockets, retrieved a green paper stub.

Deck A, Berth 4.

She made her way down through the ship. When she knocked on the cabin door she was greeted by a small, pretty blonde. The girl introduced herself and then her friend, also small but with a beakish face. Nurses, one was Peggy, the other May. They had trained together, Peggy said, and wasn't it exciting to be going away?

Violet smiled, shook hands. They were eager, polite, like excitable schoolgirls at a hockey match. They began to ask her various things, where she was from, where she had been.

A machinist!

Wales!

They ushered her in. One of them asked if she'd been to Italy before.

Before the war, she meant.

Stupid question, Violet thought.

She squeezed past them into the tiny space. A third woman was lying on the top bunk to the right. Her ankles were crossed, her hands clasped casually behind her head.

Hallo, she said.

English, Violet thought. Cut-glass. She checked for signs of rank.

No stripes, no pips.

Her name was Maggie, she said.

The cabin was hot. The two nurses fluttered about, talking with kirby grips pinched between their lips. One of them hitched up her skirt to straighten her petticoat underneath, giggling as she fished it down with one hand.

Violet slung her bag onto the bunk below Maggie's. She looked older than the other two, about Violet's age. She wore one of those side caps you could buy when your training was done. It sat at a jaunty angle on her head. Her belongings were already folded and stacked at the end of her bed.

She had dark curly hair and pale skin. Her body looked angular and lean, like a drawing in a fashion magazine.

Violet ducked her head to sit on the bottom bunk, slunk her spine, had to lean awkwardly on her side. She tried the reading lamp. It didn't work.

The girls were talking about sea legs and Atlantic storms. Old wives' tales about chewing this and that, keeping your eyes on the horizon, putting your head between your knees.

Quite without warning, Maggie swung to the floor.

She landed in one deft movement, like a gymnast off the bar.

Violet. Fancy a walk?

~

The passageways were narrow and dim. Maggie was moving swiftly towards the upper decks. Some men rounded the corner up ahead then stopped, a couple of them visibly shocked, unsure of who should let whom pass. A sergeant stepped back, broad-chested, his tunic pulled taut.

Afternoon, Sir.

Maggie clicked her heels and stood straight but there was something mocking about her face.

He flattened himself against the bulkhead and the others did the same. Then Violet felt Maggie take her hand as they edged past, sideways on. She held her breath and the sergeant turned his head yet it felt like their bodies still touched, chest to chest. When Violet glanced up, she could see that his jaw was clenched.

Feel that Pram Boy, yes?
Everybody standing to attention, erect
Feel it everywhere on board,
their long, drawn-out thirst.
In uniforms that pull at shoulders, buttocks, hips,
bodies that bulge and slip.

They moved on through the maze of the ship, Maggie still pulling Violet by the hand. At ladders or hatches she would let go, only to take it again when they reached a straight pass. She threw questions back that Violet strained to hear. Her answers came out monosyllabic, stunned. She was breathless and her feet got in the way. She felt overthrown, outraged at the same time as there was a rush, a thrill.

What kind of person expects the world to yield that way, to sway with every bend of her wiry limbs?

Come on, this way!

Somehow, they came out at the stern. The ship was already a fair way out of the port. The sea was vast, the water churned.

Maggie pushed her chest forward with her hips against the rail. Then she let out a loud trill, kicked one foot out behind and held the pose. Her lips were vivid in the cold.

Violet glanced around, embarrassed by the display but Maggie laughed and the wind whipped her hair across her face. Strands of it caught in her mouth. Then she threw her head back and shouted Violet's name.

The sound pierced the air like a knife, before the wind carried it away.

So wait, Pram Boy, wait
As your Mama turns her head,
feels butterflies instead
Chaplipped and
                spat at in the spray
All a-swell, Pram Boy
(and pretty, in her own way).

So.

You must wait until she calls
you, hauls you in
Let others glitter
            at the surface
of things.

For you, Pram Boy,
you are anchored, moored.

You
  are
    a long
      throw
        overboard.

10

Fred had been away for nearly two months. When Violet came out of the hospital she had taken one week off, then returned to munitions with the girls. They'd gone back to the same routine, Violet and Edith and Flo, friends since before the war, click-clacking across the factory floor.

They all made a big hurrah. She told them the joke about the playpen and the cot. They liked that, admired her spirit, they said.

They started at eight o'clock. Five minutes to put on your overalls and tie up your curls. The men were already trudging through in their steel-capped boots.

All right, girls?

The bell went and they moved off. Violet's job was to drill holes in valves for submarines.

Machines for machines for machines, Flo said. It never ends.

She would complain of being bored but Violet quite liked the work. And they were lucky where they were. They'd made a big fuss of them all when the women came in. Now they outnumbered the men.

When it was their turn to take a break Mr Benson would put the wireless on. They would sing, and know he was watching. He favoured Flo, all the men did, but that was part of the fun of it.

Violet looked over to her right. Flo used to be on the same line but had retrained while she was away. She glanced up and grinned, gave Violet an encouraging nod. Her features were dwarfed by a pair of enormous goggles with a black rubber rim. Violet laughed and one of the other girls started a joke, until the bell went and the sound of machinery drowned her out.

11

There were twelve women on board. An ATS officer whom they never saw, then the two nurses, a few more ATS, a couple of Wrens and one WAAF.

They ate together in C Deck mess hall with the NCOs. Each night the girls on duty would go down to the galley, collect the food and share it out. If you weren't there by six it was tough, you did without.

Most of the others were already sitting down. Violet joined the queue of soldiers filing in. A sergeant made a joke, asked her if she was there to serve dinner and what she had cooked.

She watched him coldly as he spoke, took out a cigarette.

You'll be lucky, she said under her breath.

Another one offered her a light. She leaned in slightly and he shielded the match.

Thanks.

He nodded, asked her name.

Private Davies. Sir.

She looked directly into his face. Over his shoulder she could see the nurses flapping their arms, mouthing that they'd saved her a place.

The sergeant turned and looked.

Well, Private. Better not be late.

The nurses giggled as she approached.

Hoo, Violet! Sweet on you, that one!

Violet took a long draw on her cigarette. She thought of when she was fifteen, Edwyn Lyle behind the shed at his father's shop; his darting, bird-like eyes, his dry fingers in the cold, his face when he shuddered and crumpled inside his clothes.

And so it goes, Pram Boy
Girls with their soldier boys
Mock coy though they had to check
if it was meant to be like that
– quick, painful, difficult
to get in, with him
blindly pushing
and them worrying

that it won't go
As it pokes and
bends, desperate to jab
Then when it's over, slips out.

Not me, girls, Violet said. He was asking about you two.

More laughter. The nurses were what Violet imagined boarding school was like. Green as apples, they ripened as the days went by.

Same as usual, I'm afraid.

The others were back from the galley with the food. They put the cans on the table with a thud. The metal handles clattered and they opened the lids. Everyone passed down their plates.

Violet looked around. Maggie was late. Violet craned her neck and saw that she was just outside the mess, talking to an officer they'd met the other day. He thought he knew Maggie from before. They'd been out on deck when he came over, Maggie laughing at something Violet had said.

That was how she was. *You're hiding something, Vi,* or *Violet, you're so droll.* Her fingers on her all the while.

Then the officer approached and Violet noticed the way they spoke, a change in Maggie's tone. They went through all the people and places they both might know.

Marlborough? The Haverdeans? Summer of '37 at Aix-en-Provence?

Now, Maggie was laughing as he spoke. He blew smoke into the air above her head. Her body was angled backwards, her jawline exposed. Her hand rested on his arm, her mouth an 'O'.

Dinner was a piece of thin meat with carrots and two halves of a potato. They were finished in ten minutes flat. Violet looked back to see if Maggie was going to come, if she should save her some.

But by then, Maggie was gone.

~

The nurses had a rota of suitors for cards after dinner each night.

Are you coming, Vi?

Violet shook her head, went out for some air on deck. When she got back to the cabin, Maggie was already there. The standard-issue pyjamas were loose on her frame. She looked up as Violet came in, threw her arm out over the back of the chair.

Darling Vi.

One leg was tucked up against the seat, the other lolled open to the side. Violet took off her cap and loosened the combs holding her hair back, pulled them out. Her voice was casual when she spoke.

So, Mags, who was that man?

You mean Captain Stokes?

I suppose. Blond hair, cigarette case. Funny jokes.

Maggie looked thrilled and gave a little clap.

Oh Violet. Don't be jealous.

Of who? I'm not.

Violet turned away to undress. She unbuttoned her shirt, stepped out of her skirt, rolled her stockings down. Maggie's eyes on her were sharp as knives. She felt like a pearl prised out of its shell.

With you tucked in there?
Well well well.
Hello sailor, ain't you swell?

Because with Maggie, Violet was never sure. They would be at dinner or in the cabin sorting their things and she would feel the force of her gaze, insistent, a challenge.

And Violet had watched her, too. For any sign, any hint that she may have guessed. Yet she felt better than she had all along. Strong, alert. And she held herself tight. Her height, her broad shoulders helped to conceal the slight mound of her belly sticking out.

Maggie had closed her book. It was a thick novel, the second one that Violet had seen her read. There was an officer somewhere she swapped them with. Violet held on to the upper bunk as she pulled her pyjamas on and struggled to remove her slip from underneath. Maggie watched with a doubtful expression on her face. She made no effort to look away.

Don't you want to get back to your book?

Maggie laughed, unfurled her limbs and climbed into the bed above.

Violet got into the lower bunk and pulled the blankets up. The springs of Maggie's bed creaked, the light clicked off.

~

They hadn't been asleep for long when the nurses clattered in and turned the lights back on.

Violet sat up. Peggy was drunk. There had been an altercation with a boy out on deck, May said. Peggy had gone for a stroll but there was some to-do and another soldier had heard her shout, then there had been a fight.

Maggie tutted loudly and Peggy started to cry. Her friend held her all the while by the arm, patted and preened her like a pet, arranged her hair behind her neck.

Hold on, she said. There there.

Then May kneeled down and took off Peggy's shoes, unhooked her skirt and stockings one by one. Peggy clung on to the top bunk while her friend unbuttoned her blouse, slipped the straps of her bra off her shoulders and went round to undo it from the back.

The nurse stood swaying with one hand across her chest. Her breasts were fleshy beneath her fingers and her eyes were half closed. Violet looked away as her friend looped her pyjamas over her head like catching an animal in a net, pulled her limp arms through.

They were soon asleep. Violet waited in the shadow of her bunk and stared at the slats of Maggie's bed above. She thought of the four of them all parcelled up. Safe, it felt like. Snug. She listened to the shudder of the ship, sometimes an echo from below, turned over, drifted, her breathing soft and slow.

And you Pram Boy?
Darkly stowed
Listen to the women's voices come in waves,
sob, or sing you off to sleep.
Cocooned within the belly-pit of the ship

among three other women's wombs
Feel their cycles clicking into sync
How their bodies swell, shed, bleed,
how they dream through the stop-go wetness of their loins.

There, sweet boy,
mother-lover, son-to-be.
Decked and berthed and set in the hold,
your ears are shells of tiny, soft-cell bones,
your heart a bivalve,

       open
       close.
You have fingers, and toes.

So wait then, stay your course.
That's you, mother-lover,
filling her up.
Down in the womb-glow,
sweet loving cup.

12

Every Sunday Violet went to her mother's for lunch. They'd had April showers and she'd been caught without a coat. Her feet were soaked and she'd taken her skirt off to let it dry. Elizabeth had given her one of her own.

You can keep it actually, Vi. If it fits. I've gone off it.

It was a mustard-coloured plaid thing, unlined. It was all right as long as she left the waistband unhooked.

Elizabeth sat opposite in a pale pink blouse. It had a tie at the neck and generous sleeves with deep cuffs. Her sister had just turned seventeen. She was yet to decide what her contribution to the war effort would be. Violet had no idea where she got her clothes. She had nylons to spare and a brand-new coat.

Their mother spooned out the mince, passed down the peas.

Your sister tells me she's been invited to a dance.

She shook out her napkin so that it snapped, draped it onto her lap.

At the American base, her mother said, and held Violet's gaze.

Oh! That one, yes.

Elizabeth gave her a hopeful glance. Violet had no idea but it was clear she was required to help. Flo would know one of the soldiers, no doubt, had probably been invited herself. You'd see them sometimes at The Dog, the GIs. They'd take up one whole side, buy everyone drinks, laugh louder than everyone else.

Well, Vi. She's not to go on her own.

Of course not. Sweet Elizabeth, wrapped up in a bow.

When Violet had met Fred, it was her life that had been racing ahead. It was actually Elizabeth, half drowning in the municipal baths, who had met him first. Fred had seen her struggling, dived in and hauled her to the side.

Violet had dried her off brusquely and sent her home on the bus, cross to be made a spectacle of. But she had stayed a full hour after that, sat at the side of the pool. She was sixteen. He was older. She had watched him on the high-dive, puffing out his chest. His wavy hair was pressed flat to his head as he came up through the surface and took a breath.

She felt like a pebble at the bottom of a lake, waiting to be put in his pocket. He was sturdy and strong. He laughed like a song.

Ten weeks now since he'd gone.

And it was as if she had taken two steps back. She thought of their little house up the road, the patched armchair, the drop-leaf table, quiet without either of them there. And the room upstairs, ready and waiting, the walls still bare.

No summer baby, she thought. No noise and mess.

Now there wasn't even Fred.

13

The atmosphere in the mess hall had a febrile edge.

Better line your stomachs, someone said.

There was word of a storm. A group of soldiers had got hold of some drink and were egging each other on. They reminded Violet of the men from the rugby club back home, all of them spilling out of the pub by ten, spewing into their hands, the sound of vomit spattering on the ground.

No, she didn't miss it. Land.

Violet lay quietly in her bunk. She tried to concentrate on the motion and read her body's response. Nothing so far. She hadn't been sick at all since she'd been on board.

All those times at the factory, kneeling on the concrete floor of the lav. Then during training when they were out on hikes in the moors, her throat burning with bile, dog-tired and hungry all the time.

And she thought of all the miles she had travelled since then. Just her and a tiny shell of a child. If it was real, if it was still there. In the sea and the swell. As the ship rose and fell.

Her departure had not gone down well. Her mother responded with silence and wounded pride. They didn't speak for a few days and when they did, her main concern was the shop and how she would cope.

Violet had already thought of that. She suggested they ask her cousin Aggie to come and stay. She could lend a hand for full board and half pay. She was fourteen and full of fluff but pretty and eager to please.

She'll be much better with the customers than me, Violet said.

Her mother scoffed loudly and shook her head but a few days later, Aggie arrived. She beamed like a bride, was full of questions about ribbon, wool and silk embroidery threads.

Violet's mother stopped her in her tracks. There wasn't much of that, she said. Just blackout cloth and flannelette.

With everyone else who asked though, she was gracious and contained. The butcher, the priest, the women who came into the shop as news got round.

Violet would be standing out back and hear the bell tinkle them in.

It isn't what you deserve, Anne, they would say.

As if Violet was going out there on purpose to be killed, or was already dead. Like poor old Edwyn Lyle, shot in the neck.

All that grief had gone to their heads.

And Violet's mother was an expert in that, long before the war. A grimly determined widow, she was reserved and quiet. It was part of the dignity all her friends admired.

Violet would breeze through, then. Wilfully cheerful, bright.

Morning Mrs Owen.

Morning, Vi.

And they would watch her carefully and after a while say they'd heard the news about her going away. Then add, You're brave! As if it was a new phase or fad. As if you wouldn't catch their daughters doing something like that. Then they would all smile and nod, and later probably remark on how they found her a bit odd.

~

Violet woke to hull creak and sick smells.

Peggy had started first, groaning out pale lumps into her lap. Then May was caught by the clamour and sat up, her vomit trickling down the wall from above.

Violet turned on the light.

Maggie wasn't there.

Look, Pram Boy,
see the mermaid brushing her long dark hair?
Silvery tail, snatches of song,
                    now gone!

Peggy was down from her bunk, stumbling each time the ship lurched. Violet stood further down holding on to the rail.

Then Peggy fell, grabbed on.

Violet pulled on her tunic then managed her shoes. She glanced back as she opened the door.

Sorry girls.

The passageways were slippy and foul. Violet was thrown in a zig-zag path, groping along the walls.

Out she crawls, Pram Boy

drawn by glimmers on the rocks
up, up
               Feel her tossed this way and that,
now frothed at in the foam.

She is a ship, wrecked,
far from home.

It wasn't much better further up. A few men who
weren't sick had come up to congregate in small groups.
They stood around the grand staircase holding on, or
crouched in corners attempting to play cards. Others
came rushing through and scrambled to get out on deck,
some of them helped by friends holding on to their
clothes.

Violet groped her way along holding on to the bulkhead
ropes. A soldier stepped away to let her pass, offering his
hip flask as a joke.

She found a quiet place near the hull and sat on the floor
with her knees up, feet planted down. She felt her pockets with one hand.

Matches but no cigarettes.

She tried to catch a soldier's eye and watched him
weave across the parquet floor, but he squeezed himself
behind a beam, rolled up his tunic as a pillow and went
to sleep.

Violet grasped up at the rope with her hand. All her muscles strained to stay upright as the ship lunged. She was alert like a cat.

Violet!

Maggie was walking towards her, smiling as the motion sent her stumbling like a drunk.

There you are!

She was wearing her pyjamas with a man's tunic that was far too large. Her feet were bare. Violet looked at her in slight alarm.

Don't be ridiculous Violet, they're sick as hell up there.

They had to shout above the squall. Maggie sat down next to her on the floor.

It's best to keep your eyes on the horizon, she said.

Violet gave a derisive snort.

They were quiet for a while. Violet knew where Maggie had been. In the preening arms of Captain Stokes, or another one like him. They all seemed the same to her. Nodded politely to all the girls, asked your name and where you were from, claimed to know someone from there, or somewhere near.

Officer class. Each one more dreary and accomplished than the last.

Violet yawned. Every so often a door flew open and a soldier crawled back in. The storm was subsiding. Maggie leaned her head against Violet's arm.

They sat there, supporting one another's weight.

Maggie?

Yes.

Where have you sailed to? Violet asked.

And Maggie began to tell her. After her schooling, Venice, Florence, Sienna, Rome. Then Greece and the Levant. Some of the war she'd spent in Egypt, then in France.

Violet was further than she'd ever been from home. And the war would soon be over, someone said.

She leaned her head against Maggie's, closed her eyes. She was so tired, her words came out slurred.

What about Naples? What's it like?

I've heard it's beautiful and bold and filthy and wrecked.

Violet opened her eyes, glanced down to the side. Maggie grinned.

You'll love it, Vi.

14

It took two bus rides to get to the American base.

Flo and Edith were like excited schoolgirls on the top deck but Elizabeth sat quietly, her hands in her lap. She was wearing her green crêpe dress.

Flo was in red. She was so perfect and small. Violet had always been bigger-boned but Flo was light as a feather. It made men want to pick her up like a doll. Violet had seen her physically carried away before. Nights like this or New Year's Eve, or after the local team had won a match.

Violet had opted for a skirt and blouse.

The dance was in a prefab hut with mint-green walls. She'd imagined high ceilings and banners and flags, but there was none of that. Soldiers were lined up at the bar passing drinks back over their heads. A few girls sat on chairs round the edge of the room, sucking on straws in bottles of pop.

The swing band started up. Violet thought she wouldn't mind a dance. Someone had already asked Flo so Edith signalled and they pushed their way further into the room. Some of the men stepped aside and doffed their caps. Then Flo came back with her GI and he grinned and shook their hands, introduced his friends.

They were like that, the Americans.

One of the soldiers was talking to Elizabeth but she was distracted, scanning the room. Violet intervened. He was making jokes about how they ate biscuits with gravy, squash and okra and grits. She laughed at the names, noticed her voice change, become more English.

When she looked round, Elizabeth's posture had changed.

There was a soldier pushing towards them through the crowd. It was as if they had turned off the lights, and only Elizabeth glowed.

His name was Antonio, Tony for short.

Italian, Elizabeth said. From New Jersey, which was near New York.

Edith came over to join them, intrigued. They made another round of hellos and the GI stood on his tip-toes and beckoned to someone at the bar to bring them some drinks.

Yes, Violet could see it now. They all had the same dark hair and skin. She looked around the room, there were groups of them here and there.

Well. Whatever they were, the Americans, they were always well-turned-out.

Violet tried to imagine Fred like that. And Tommy and Frank and Jack. Some of them were a bit rough, a bit brusque. But that didn't stop them having a laugh. They worked hard. And Fred had his stripes.

The pace of the music had slowed and Tony pulled Elizabeth away to dance. There was a handsome GI with a girl who was surprisingly plain. Thick ankles, mousy hair. Kept looking down at the floor. Violet scanned the room, saw a glint of Elizabeth's dress. Then they moved into view and she glanced over Tony's shoulder, gave her a little wave.

15

It was early, Violet was out on deck. The sky was still tinged with pink. They had sailed through the Strait of Gibraltar a few days before and now the sun was gently warm on her face. She took off her tunic and rolled up her sleeves.

On land, back home, Violet would have been watching for spring. The valleys would be shaggy and soaked, like a drenched fur coat. But there would be primroses at the roadside by now, new lambs.

The sea stretched out before her as if there was nothing beyond, as if it would always be there.

She wished she could stay like that, with everything else washed out. She had tried to plan, to think ahead, to guess how much time she had left. Another month? Six weeks? Before she really began to show. Before there were rumours, or it was obvious. Before she declared herself and was sent home.

Would she be sent home?

Violet looked at her watch. It was nearly eight o'clock. Time for breakfast then roll call, inspection then drill. She rolled down her sleeves, put her tunic back on.

She took a deep breath, shaded her eyes from the sun.

And there it was. Land. Italy. Violet felt her stomach flutter. Hunger? No, that wasn't it.

She paused. A kick.

There was a ripple, then gone. Now again, beneath her ribs.

A flip, a tail fin's dip.

Like something slipping out of her grip.

There, Pram Boy, you are a disappearing fish
So lick your lips, sip her fluid,
suck your thumb.

Come, come.

Pram Boy, pill-boy, pearl of the sea
Feel your Mama touch her belly as she says,

Come with me.

With the light all pink
on gunmetal grey
Taking a turn about the deck,
a glance, a cigarette

Feel your Mama take a long, deep breath.

There.

Fret no more.

The end of a voyage at the end of a war.
Hush now, Pram Boy, you were carried after all.

PART THREE

16

Into the heat and stench of disorder, they disembarked.

A bang, a jeering,
a leer from a small boy grimed with sweat;

Port-surge, shit-smell, something slippy underfoot
(fruit-rot, cabbage leaf, gobs of spit).

Can you feel it, Pram Boy?
Can you march in time?
A change, a hardening,
        the jarring of the solid ground as she treads,
gets her pockets picked.

There is the smell of diesel oil and fish.

And the women!
Faces flickering,
sent skittering like foals across the flags,
sweat-necked and whinnying in the crowd.
All those white girls,
the startled pale and bright girls,
snagged on the stares of balcony women dressed in black.

Quick! March!

And your Mama, Pram Boy,
yeasty in her private parts.

The Staff Sergeant was ahead. She had ordered them into a column of twos. She was red in the face, gesturing sternly to hold the line. Someone pushed past and Violet nearly fell into the girl behind.

The port was a murmur, a mass. Men surged forward, they were grabbed at and passed along by a human tide; men acrid and close, wearing clothes from twenty years ago, clothes that had soaked up sweat that dried in rings.

The nurses had been ordered to fall in with the ATS. They were up ahead. Violet watched as they were jostled and shoved. A man sniffed close to the pretty one's face, laughed, groped at her chest.

Finally they reached an open space. The Staff Sergeant signalled for them to stop, regroup.

Breathless, nobody moved or spoke. Violet blinked, wiped her upper lip. They were in battledress and the canvas was hot and stiff. Maggie was directly in front but hadn't turned round. There were strands of hair stuck to the nape of her neck. They looked like someone had licked them there, wet.

Mags!

She turned.

This is stupid, Maggie rasped. Why couldn't they send transport to pick us up?

Violet shrugged.

They started up again and fell into step. They marched past warehouses and huts. Women with fish guts wiped on their thighs laughed and pointed with their knives. Violet's ankle went over for the second time.

They began to climb up a series of narrow streets. Clothes and yellowing bed sheets hung between the houses up above. The shade was cooler but the air was stagnant, thick. They passed doorways and women standing with babies in their arms, braless in scant clothes, or else older and squat. A boy came down the hill on a bicycle and gestured crudely as he passed.

When they emerged it was onto an avenue with motor cars and Army personnel. The sun was high, the buildings were bright in stone that shot it back, white pillars crumbling and pocked. They marched for a while in the shade of a promenade. More women in doorways, heavily made-up. There were shut-up shops, then men with wagons full of fruit and veg. The girl next to Violet tripped up and Violet caught her by the elbow but kept looking ahead.

The ATS officer led them to a white palazzo with a courtyard in a circular sweep. All the palm trees had ragged leaves.

At ease, ladies. Bravo.

She turned and saluted the soldiers standing to attention at the gate, then disappeared through a tall arch. The soldiers relaxed. The column of women collapsed.

~

The boarding house was on the next street. An old woman let them into a small courtyard with a well, took up a broom and started conspicuously to sweep. There were a few old bicycles leaned up against a wall, a washing line with underwear hanging limp and drab.

Maggie looked askance, Violet caught her eye and laughed.

Cracked plaster walls, tiled floor. There were mosquito nets knotted above each bed tied to wooden beams overhead.

The billet was all ATS. The nurses had been ordered to wait behind, they would join units heading north. They were tearful, made a round of little goodbyes.

Some of the other bunks were already made up. There were photographs tacked onto the wall around each one. Maggie peered closely at them all, looked under pillows, opened drawers.

Violet unrolled her cot as swiftly as she could. She unpacked her kit and laid her khaki drills out flat. She'd been issued them at camp in York, weeks back. A sergeant had come with a list and watched them file through the quartermaster's stores. As each woman approached he'd shout whether they should be large, medium or small. Violet was large, on account of her height. Now she looked at the pale sand-coloured cotton, the flaps of the pockets square and stiff.

Yes. They would still fit.

Maggie had chosen a bed by the door and sat stripped down to her underwear. She had her chin on her chest rubbing her back and neck, then crossed her legs to knead her calf. She looked like a dancer off the stage.

Perhaps she was, Violet thought. Maggie could have been anyone before so how would she ever know? It was difficult to tell what was real and what was for show.

Maggie exhaled loudly and flopped back, her limbs spread out in a star.

Violet! I'm fagged.

She closed her eyes. Violet watched as her chest rose and fell. You could see the shape of her ribs and the concave dip of her stomach between her hips.

She thought of the ship, the cabin, the fug of their shared body heat.

There were four washstands with a jug and bowl at each. Violet unbuttoned the stiff cloth down to her waist and shrugged out of the sleeves. She splashed her face and stood for a moment to feel the water evaporate into the air.

Her skin cooled down, and Violet sensed herself contract almost, retreat.

What had she done? Coming so far from home.

She thought of the soldier. She used to touch the creases around his eyes. He would sweep her hair to the side with his delicate hands.

But that was all gone. He was back in Aberdeen.

Violet looked around the room. Maggie was asleep.

17

Violet sat in her mother's kitchen chopping rhubarb for a pie.

She scattered the pieces into the dish and sprinkled sugar over the top, licking it off her fingers as she went.

She had been thinking about Elizabeth's new coat.

It was the same colour as the rhubarb in the dish. Impossible to miss.

Violet left the kitchen and went upstairs to the bedroom they used to share. The coat was on the back of the door. It was made from a thick gabardine but was light enough for spring. The lining was a paler pink. Violet took it down and put it on.

No. No good.

The coat was too small. Elizabeth it transformed, she seemed to glide around in its embrace.

Violet took the coat off and hung it back on the door. She

lingered by the dresser, put the lid on a jar of cream.

There were little figurines lined up in a row, ballet dancers and such. They needed a dust. On the bed, various items were cast aside from where Elizabeth had tried them on. A blouse and a skirt. A brand-new pair of nylons.

Violet picked them up and trailed them through her hands. So fine they were barely there. The thread caught on the rough skin of her thumb.

Violet opened a drawer to put them away and saw a small rectangular box pushed right to the back. She had to flatten a pile of hankies to get it out. Inside was a ring. It was a thin gold band with tiny diamonds in the shape of a flower.

She hadn't seen this coming, not at all. Tony from New Jersey, nearly New York. She had assumed he'd just go back and that would be that.

Violet stared at the ring. The ring stared back. She resisted the urge to try it on.

All those charming things he brought her. Flowers, fancies, food they had never seen. Then she had turned up in that coat, pleased as punch, their mother inspecting the buttons, turning the seams over for faults.

It was just her colour, everyone said.

Give us a twirl.

That's our girl.

Violet put the ring back in its box. The lid shut with a hollow snap.

~

Downstairs, the rhubarb had turned a crackled brown. Violet fetched the pastry from the pantry and threw some flour onto the tabletop.

It was as if Elizabeth had won the game and Violet was stuck. Even though she was the eldest, married and settled in her own home.

She rolled out an oval disc, cracked an egg into a cup.

It was no longer about patience, or hard work, or joining up.

She brushed the edges of the dish and slung the pastry down flat, then made a hole in the top with a short, sharp stab.

No, she thought, it had always been like that. Elizabeth would sail off in that coat, and never look back.

18

The British Army HQ occupied the whole of the palazzo. It was faded and in disrepair with sandbags at the gates, metal blockades and some windows on the ground floor boarded up.

They had been there for two weeks. The ATS girls worked Monday to Friday from eight until four. They'd walk the short distance to HQ each day, past the vendors with their carts, pestered by children in tattered clothes.

Violet strode on until Maggie caught her up. She'd bought a bag of apricots and cherries and ate them as she went, spitting the stones into the street.

Here, Vi, try these.

She placed a handful of cherries in Violet's palm. They were small and sweet and the juice was shockingly red.

They arrived at the palazzo and went straight up. Their office was in a white-painted, high-ceilinged hall on the upper floor. It had ornate stucco plasterwork and tall windows running along one side. The typists sat at the front with the rest of them in neat little rows behind.

For this is how it was, Pram Boy,
light divided from shade in hard, clean lines.

Some of the girls lingered at the windows finishing their
cigarettes. The soldiers crossing below knew to look up.

See how they shield their eyes, Pram Boy,
then don't;
And the girls dab their foreheads, click
their compact mirrors shut,
only to open them again five minutes later.

Violet took a file from the tray as the typewriters began
their clatter.

And you there, growing fatter down below,
work-shy, cockeyed
and everything in rods or rows
to keep the slack ooze in
(the heat, the streets, the gore of wounds still coming in)

For this is how it was, Pram Boy,
women close-quartered with each other.

Friendships formed, lovers were distracted from their letters.

A girl called Mary was late. She blustered up from behind
and knocked Violet's elbow as she passed.

Sorry, Vi.

She dabbed the sweat from her forehead with her hand-kerchief and heaved a dramatic sigh. If this was late April, what would it be like in July?

Violet turned and smiled.

Hot, I should think, Mary.

The girl tucked a strand of lank hair behind her ear.

Anyway, the war will be over by then.

I should bloody well hope so, someone else said.

Violet wasn't sure of her name but she'd been there longer than anyone else. She told vivid stories about attacks in the street, locals eating stray cats for meat.

Just you wait. A little bit hotter and the mosquitoes will be out.

A chair scraped loudly at the back of the room. The Staff Sergeant got up and walked purposefully around.

Violet kept her head down.

Vi!

Maggie sat two rows behind to Violet's left. She was paired off with a girl called Beth whom she had dismissed after the first day. She talked too much, Maggie said. Kept asking for help.

She made a gesture behind the sergeant's back and rolled her eyes. She tried to slide a pencil behind her ear like the men in the factory did but it kept slipping so she took it out, tapped it impatiently on the desk instead.

I'm so bored! she mouthed.

Violet shook her head, opened the logbook on her desk. It was easy work, all of them were Pay Clerks. Some of the girls talked about the soldiers as if they knew them well. It was all there in the files: age, the colour of their eyes, their hair, their height. Some of them let their imaginations run wild. They knew which men were married or whose wives were expecting a child. There were medical forms, promotions and fines. Sometimes, one of them died of his wounds or was killed.

~

They went to the NAAFI after work for a drink. It was in the Royal Palace down by the port. Violet had already described it to Aggie in a letter home. Every one of the rooms had marble floors, ornate panels and doors, carved ceilings and chandeliers. There were films and shows, dances in the ballroom every weekend.

Maggie hadn't joined them there at all. When Violet asked her why, she just shrugged. Had her own friends, she said, preferred to spend time with them instead.

Violet made her way through the grand hall with the others. There was something about being in a building so cavernous and tall. Not like church but something bigger, built for men. She thought it would make her feel small but it had the opposite effect. She walked faster to hear the sharp clip of her brogues on the smooth stone steps.

They arrived at the tea room, which had a terrace giving on to some gardens down below. They pulled chairs into the last of the day's sun. By now there were a few sailors coming in. One of the girls went to fetch a jug of lemonade. There was never much sugar, they drank it and shuddered, pursed and smacked their lips.

Violet watched as the others sat back, stretched out their legs. She was conscious of her blouse pulling tight across her chest, her waistband digging in.

It was only later, in the evenings, when it grew cool and she walked alone through the city streets, that she would feel her body relax. Muscles slovenly and slack felt strong again. She didn't mind the noise or the din, felt fluid, taking it all in. She passed hawkers with their wares, leave-takers, whores and spivs. Young men stared from beaded doorways, licked their lips.

Right girls, I'm off.

Violet stood up, hooked her finger under her watch to stretch it away from the skin.

The girls let her go, joking about her being a dark horse – all those long walks – or else being a bore, always the first one back to the dorm. She laughed, let them carry on, left them shouting something after she'd gone.

She stopped at the American snack bar to buy a sandwich on her way out and walked eating from the brown paper bag. She emerged onto the street and turned left. Next to the Palace was the opera house. Young boys hung about to catch an officer for a cigarette. Then Violet looked up and her breath caught in her throat. She swallowed. Maggie was just ahead.

Fine-drawn limbs, dark hair, standing among a group of well-dressed men.

She was in civilian clothes and Violet had to check again to make sure that it was her. She wore wide black slacks with pleats at the hips and a black silk blouse. It was high at the neck, draped across her throat and chest. Then she turned and Violet saw that it plunged down at the back.

She ducked into the shadow of a shut-up stall. She was so close she could almost hear Maggie talk.

Was it Italian? Yes. But now, addressing another of the men, perhaps French.

Violet stood and watched. After a while another man joined the group. He was tall with sharp features and narrow eyes. Maggie shook his hand and then the mood seemed to shift. He didn't smile but stiffly nodded his head. He turned to Maggie and offered her his arm.

The opera. Of course.

Violet watched as they disappeared through the revolving doors.

She looked down. The sandwich was limp in its greasy paper in her hands. Feeling sick, she stuffed it into her bag, wiped a string of melted cheese from her chin.

She couldn't work it out. In the day Maggie would wink and be coy, linking arms, making her feel that they were part of the same charming act. And once or twice in the dorm, when everyone else was asleep, Violet had thought she could feel her standing by her bed, fogged by the mosquito net.

That was it, she thought, Maggie haunted, led you on. And when you reached out to touch her, pouf! She was gone.

19

Violet wasn't sure where Flo was. Edith had left hours ago. She should have known. It was nearly midnight and they'd been out since lunch. It had been treaties and pacts for days so they'd all had a chance to prepare by the time VE Day was declared.

Someone pushed past her in the crowd, moving her sharply aside, almost lifting her clear from the ground.

A soldier. Drunk.

He shunted into another group of soldiers nearby and they set him on his feet, patted his chest and turned him round like a game of blind man's bluff.

They'd walked into town from the pub. It had been great fun early on, they'd had a dance like girls on a chorus line, kicking their legs out in time. Someone had put a carnation in Violet's hair, everyone laughing along. But now she was alone and her feet ached, the night air was chill. She pulled her cardigan across her chest.

Should have left while the going was good.

She waited for the bus on Colmore Row. The ground was covered with flags and streamers and God knows what. People were sitting around on the pavements, men but a few women too. A couple of them had children in tow, curled up asleep under their coats.

There was a young man with his mouth full of pork pie. He was standing with a group of others, unsteady on his feet.

Cheer up love! How about it? Give yer one for victory?

His friends laughed. Some girls watched without a word. Violet folded her arms tighter and moved off.

Oi! I served in France, I did!

All this mess, Violet thought. And the men with their slurred mouths spitting crumbs and filth. And the women wearing soldiers' caps. Victory in Europe. Now they just had to clean up.

And what about Fred? No one mentioned Japan. There was no pact that meant Fred was coming home. That was all too far away for anyone here. And Fred was too far away to be any use to her.

Violet shifted her weight to the other foot, was tempted to close her eyes. She felt so deeply tired of everything.

The last bus finally arrived. People clumped together to board. Violet made her way to the back, brushed the seat and sat down.

At the next stop some soldiers got on. She recognised some of them. Flo was courting a boy from the Ninth and they'd come to the Arms the other night. One of them, John, had bought her a drink.

Violet sat up in her seat and smoothed her hair under her hat. The soldier swung forward.

Violet!

She wasn't sure if it was the bus or if he was stumbling because he was drunk. She'd been tipsy herself but it had worn off. She laughed.

John! Can you rescue me please? I've lost Flo.

He gave a little nod, sat down and shuffled up.

My pleasure. Can't have you travelling home on your own. Which is your stop?

The bus took a sharp bend and they held on to the seat in front. Thuds and cheers came from the top deck.

That's your lot, Violet said.

John shook his head as if the soldiers were children playing up. He had a kind face. In the pub the other night they'd played four hands on a few tunes. He sang quite well. Now they talked about how it was when people knew you could play, how they'd never let you stop. There'd been drinks lined up all along the top of the piano by the end of the night.

They were quiet for a while. Violet watched the buildings go by. Some were half demolished, others bomb sites. There were sides ripped off others, you could see the wallpaper flapping in the wind.

Violet turned back to say something but John had his eyes closed. He swayed slightly in the motion, still holding on to the seat in front. Every time the bus went round a corner, their arms touched.

Gently, Violet leaned against his side. She felt herself nodding off, then her head would jolt up. Then she slipped her hand through John's arm, let her head rest on his shoulder. His body shifted, his hand resting lightly on her knee. Then she felt the weight of him relax as he breathed out and leaned in.

20

Violet was surprised when Maggie invited her out to the coast. At the weekends she usually went off with her friends, or that was what Violet assumed. Then she'd come back and talk about all places that Violet should see. Pompeii, or the Americans on Capri. As if she was on holiday. As if she could go there for free.

But when Maggie told her about the cove she was eager to go. Since VE day the city had felt leaden and slow. It was still only May but the heat sat like a vapour in the streets.

Some soldiers gave them a lift. They had a battered old jeep with doors that opened the wrong way round. Violet sat in the back, Maggie was up front. The driver chewed gum and drove too fast, looking at Maggie whenever he could.

They dropped them at a bend in the road. There was nothing but clifftop and scrubland. The heat sang.

The path down to the cove was rocky and steep but Maggie stepped nimbly ahead. She wore her regulation shirt tied in a knot at the front and a pair of khaki shorts that were far too big.

Violet followed behind, carrying the bag with the food.

Maggie's friends were ahead of them, sitting on the shore. There was an American GI and an Italian girl. The soldier stood up and shook her hand. His name was Jeremiah but most people called him Jim. He was from a division based out of town he said, and winked. Violet didn't understand. Segregated, he meant. One place for whites, another for them. Violet wasn't sure what to say but he laughed anyway, then the Italian girl leaned forward and kissed Maggie on each cheek.

The GI stepped back politely. Violet asked him how long he had been there, where in the US he was from.

Atlanta, Georgia, he said. How 'bout you, Violet?

She told him Wales, he looked unsure.

A little country next door to England, Maggie said.

She'd been quiet until then, a piece of dried grass between her teeth. She flashed a smile, turned over a pebble with her foot.

Nella was the girl. She wore a yellow bathing suit and a wide-brimmed hat. Her English was without fault. Her family was from Naples, she said, but she went to school abroad. She sat down on a woven mat that was the same as the basket by her side, unwrapped a piece of hard cheese and ate thin slices from the blade of a knife.

They chatted about the city, the end of the war, what they were going to do now.

Ship out! said Jeremiah and laughed. Nella made a sad face, leaned over and kissed his arm. His division were running trips while they were waiting to be demobbed. He'd been to Vesuvius, he said, bought a nickel stuck in a piece of molten rock for a dollar. He laughed again, the sweat on his forehead glistening in the sun.

We're going to stay on, aren't we, Vi?

Maggie was more animated now. Violet shrugged. It looked like they could. On VE Day there had been fireworks and a band, the Palace and gardens crammed with hundreds of men. But they'd gone back to work as usual the next day and nothing at all had changed.

Still lots to do here, the Staff Sergeant said, prowling among the desks. Violet commiserated with the others at lunch but was so relieved she could barely eat.

They were quiet for a while. Nella lay down and closed her eyes. Her limbs were languid and honeyed and brown. The GI had taken off his shirt and stretched out by her side. His trousers had been cut short and rolled up tight around his thighs. They looked like they had been washed in the sea and dried in the sun a thousand times.

Violet tried not to stare. The contours of his body were solid and hard, from his jawbone to his shoulders, across his bare chest, his muscular arms and legs.

She looked away. Lots of the GIs were black, but she had never seen anyone like that.

She took off her shoes and socks, lit a cigarette. She could hear the hum of crickets in the grass up above. Maggie had wandered off towards the sea. The light on the waves seemed to cut into her frame where she stood at the water's edge. She shimmered, diamond-shaped.

Violet shielded her eyes with her hand and watched as Maggie threw her clothes down onto the beach. She was wearing a bright blue bathing costume underneath. She stretched her arms behind her neck to tie the straps in a bow. There were pale lines on her skin where the sun had made its mark. On another day, perhaps, with others looking on.

Maggie turned and smiled, made a little flourish with her hands. Violet stubbed her cigarette out in the stones.

Go on then, show us what it can do!

Jeremiah sat up and whistled and clapped, then Nella raised her head and looked out from beneath her hat. She gave a gleeful shout.

Che bella, Maggie!

Violet laughed, shook her head in disbelief.

Maggie dived under a wave. The white of her body flashed like a fish.

Oh Pram Boy, see?
See your Mama there,
lips parted, direct stare.
And though she is flinty and tough, your Mama,
something muscular about her manner,
she longs to be touched.

So let her lie back, recline
as she softly draws the light
Here, the epic skies
                    the ochre-glow, the bronze,
                            the burnish and
                                    the rot.

And you? Tut tut.
You are a seed
sown in the deep dark woods
                    but grown

Oh! grown,
        in the sun.

~

The others took their leave as the sun reached its peak. When they had gone, Maggie persuaded Violet to swim in the sea.

Violet stripped down to her petticoat and waded in, up to her waist, up to her chest. Her slip ballooned about her then went heavy and dragged. She slid under, came up sleek and black, her hair slicked back.

After, when they'd had more to eat, lain in the sun; when the salty residue was dry on their skin, they told each other a little about their lives. Before the war, where they grew up. Maggie's mother had died when she was a child.

My father, too.

There you go, Vi.

Maggie smiled, behind her the turquoise sea.

My dead mother, your dead father. We're meant to be.

It was late when they climbed back up to the road and Maggie stood waiting to hitch a ride. Violet's shoulders were red, her lips blistered from the sun.

Maggie, too, looked dishevelled and wild. Like an unruly, hungry child.

~

Some soldiers dropped them at the port. No questions asked, one of them said. Maggie laughed.

Violet's hips ached, her back was stiff. They'd missed dinner and soon it would be dark. It was Saturday night and the others would be at the Palace, wondering where she was.

Maggie pulled her on through the boatyard where the fishermen had their shacks. Violet was wrecked and hot, pot-bellied. Her clothes felt scratchy and stiff. Her skirt sat high above her waist, tight around her ribs. She couldn't be bothered to hold herself in.

Maggie pointed the way.

Do you ever stop? Violet sighed.

They found a place selling food from a hole in the wall. Violet stuffed the warm bread in her mouth, tasted oil and salt. Maggie shared hers, bright red with tomato paste spread thinly on top. She watched Violet eat.

What?

Here, I'll get us something to drink.

They sat on a low wall in a part of the port Violet had never seen. Heavyset women packed up the last of the day's catch. They scrubbed their benches in circles, swilled out buckets and pails, dirt under their fingernails.

Violet sniffed, wiped her nose on the back of her hand. Then Maggie stood and stretched her arms theatrically in the air. They were pale underneath, her elbows sticking sharply out to the sides. Her hair fell about her face in thick, dark curls.

Come on then, Vi. You can be my girl.

~

The tavern was in a far corner of the port. They ducked through a low door and Maggie pulled Violet on through the crowd. They found a table near the band on seats that were upturned crates. Maggie fanned her face with her hand.

It was mainly civilians, young men in vests. Some sailors, some soldiers. They leaned against pillars watching women or each other. There were thin, teenage girls, dark corners where condensation dripped down walls. A figure in a three-piece suit, slight and smooth-skinned, smoking a cheroot. Violet watched, they stared back. Violet smiled and they held her gaze. She looked away.

Maggie, I'm not sure we should stay.

The air was suffocatingly close, Violet made a gesture that she wanted to go but Maggie clicked her fingers for one of the bar girls to bring them a drink. The one who came over was plump in a day dress with buttons up the front. The top few were undone and you could see her damp flesh, her underarms stained with sweat.

The wine was warm and faintly fizzy on Violet's tongue. The dance floor was full. Everyone seemed to know what to do. They danced together and then left each other alone, moved their bodies apart then close.

Ciao, Maggie, Violetta!

Nella was pushing towards them through the crowd. She sent three kisses into the air and sat down. Her hair was sculpted immaculately in waves around her face. She had a different kind of drink to everyone else.

Jeremiah was still making his way across. He clasped shoulders, shook hands, nodded to the musicians as he passed.

Hey, Violet! You made it back.

She liked him, he was easy-going, relaxed. He reached over and pulled her up to dance. They moved awkwardly at first. The music was jagged, odd. He spun her away then pulled her back and she could feel him breathing in then hotly out. Then for a while he let her go. Slowly, she moved her arms, her body swayed, she let her eyes close. The GI slumped and his head hung low, his shoulders moving in rhythm, his fingers clicking with the slide of the trombone.

~

They stayed at the club until it was nearly dawn. On the walk home, Violet leaned on Maggie's arm.

She felt like her body would give in. Soft and limp.

And there was Maggie, who was lithe and quick and thin. Like one of those darting, Neapolitan boys scavenging on the street.

The flash of a coin, the clatter of bins.

Violet wanted to tell her, then. She wanted to lay it all down. All the fleshy weight of her bones but also the wakening sense of her own self. Who she was, what she had done. She didn't have long. September, the baby would come.

They turned a corner along a promenade. Violet's feet ached.

There was a woman coming towards them. Her lips were a garish red in the flickering lights.

She slowed down as they passed her but Maggie quickened their pace. The woman looped back to walk their way.

Ciao bella, come stai?

She seemed to know Maggie by name but came up on Violet's side. She was acrid with sweat and Violet could smell the alcohol on her breath.

Maggie tried to brush her off and she swayed but kept on going, draped her arm around Violet's neck. Violet could feel her bony fingers around her shoulders and down her back, then Maggie turned and slapped the woman's hand away.

Something dropped to the ground – Violet's purse. It flipped open on the cobbles, there was a faint trickle of coins and the woman seemed coiled ready to pounce. All in a moment, Maggie stepped close to the woman's face. With the clear flash of a blade Violet saw her flick open a small knife.

The woman backed away with a clumsy, gaping laugh.

Va bene, va bene, Maggie, calmati!

Maggie stepped away, the knife was nowhere to be seen. Then she grasped the woman sharply by the arm and whispered something close between clenched teeth, letting go with a shove. The woman sloped off like a wounded dog.

~

Maggie stormed on. She was muttering something, shaking her head. Violet wasn't sure if she was angry with her or talking to herself. Then she spun round.

You see? This is why I keep myself to myself.

Violet was out of breath.

Mags, I don't want to know. I don't care.

Maggie laughed, a harsh, rasping sound.

Well, Vi. I suppose we all have something to hide.

She was wild-eyed, the tendons in her neck stuck out. They were standing in the middle of the cobbled street.

Well? Do you think no one's noticed?

Violet felt her face flicker and crack. It felt like plaster falling from a wall, a thin façade shattered on the floor. Maggie turned and stalked away.

Her shoulder blades, her sharp, agile frame.

Violet had lost any sense of where they were. She looked

around her. Feral cats in rubbish heaps, or rats. Piles of rubble, wire and brick. Yet she felt like she might curl up in a ball right there and go to sleep.

Maggie came back.

To say something cruel, Violet thought. To say what she knew.

But then she came closer. Closer still. Then her hand was grasping Violet's jaw, tilting it to the side. Violet nearly stumbled, stepped back against a wall. Maggie's body met her own, pushed into it as she pushed back and Maggie kissed her on the mouth. Now Violet's head was back and Maggie was kissing her neck, Violet's hand in her hair. Then the soft press of their breasts, her round belly and Maggie's sharp hips.

There.

There, there.

Tonight, Pram Boy,
you are a caged bird
fluttering between.
Cloth-thrown, unseen,
waiting to sing your song.

Heavy in her belly,
a lover in her lap.

Lying there ready,
tap tap tap.

So sing a song of sixpence,
a pocket full of rye.
You are four and twenty blackbirds,
baked in a pie.

21

Violet waited for news from Fred. In the weeks since VE Day only two letters had got through. There was still fighting going on, he said. Still problems with supply, leeches and mosquitoes, ration packs with damp cigarettes.

Violet sat on the train watching the telegraph poles fly past. Elizabeth sat opposite. She was wearing a brand-new hat. Violet watched her. Good posture.

The wedding had been a bit of a rush. Tony had been demobbed within a week, quicker than anyone expected. He promised to send for Elizabeth straight away but it had taken a month. They waited and waited. Everyone was relieved when her papers came.

The train pulled into Southampton and they stepped out onto the platform. Elizabeth waved to a porter for help. Two of them came at once. The departure hall was vast and the tannoy blared. They waited for tourist class to be called. Elizabeth was talking about all the things that Tony said they would have. A Frigidaire, a sewing machine.

Vi? Are you listening?

Elizabeth, with her arched brows, her slightly upturned nose. She had the calm, considered air of having got further than anyone else. Violet nodded, straightened the brooch on her sister's lapel. The American had bought her that as well.

In the end their goodbyes were oddly rushed. Elizabeth was beckoned forward into another queue. Violet accompanied her, dragging her trunk, but it was taken by a porter and passed through a gate, then Elizabeth was ushered through to a turnstile up ahead.

She turned back against the flow to take Violet's hand and say goodbye. Briefly, she looked like the little girl she had always been, her expression faintly needy, pleading. Then someone pushed past and Elizabeth tutted loudly, made a haughty remark.

Well then, Violet said.

She looked into her face again, tried to find some recognition of what had passed, everything they had shared until now. But Elizabeth was composed, any moment of weakness had gone.

It took a while to spot her from down on the dock. Violet had found a place to stand with the others bidding farewell. Meanwhile her sister had got herself onto an upper deck of the ship and stood at the front of the crowd, right at the rail.

The liner was bigger but uglier than Violet expected. Not glamorous at all. There were rusty stains and bolted sheets of metal at the hull.

Violet signalled with both arms above her head and Elizabeth saw her and waved. The breeze caught her briefly and she grabbed onto her hat.

The departure was painfully slow. The liner was towed out with its horn blaring, people down below spasmodically cheering, faint whistles from above. Violet was tired, her face ached with smiling. Yet Elizabeth kept waving. In her last glimpse before the slow turn of the ship blotted her out, she didn't look like somebody leaving. She looked like somebody desperate to come back.

22

A few of the ATS women were kept on. Violet volunteered and Maggie was transferred to another part of HQ. They saw each other at lunch or in the dorm but they hadn't been out since the night at the port.

There were only a few of them left at dinner each day. Violet ate hungrily and took her empty plate to the kitchens. She could sense the others watch her return. She said nothing, sat down to await the appropriate moment to leave.

You in for rummy tonight, Vi?

Not me, Lily.

She was a tall, skinny girl from Nottingham with flat vowels and a laconic drawl. Violet had never joined them in the games room after dinner. She disliked the spectacle of the girls coyly showing their cards, taking bad advice from corporals, giggling when they lost.

Right. Too tired, I suppose.

The others looked up from their plates. Violet smiled thinly.

That's right, Lily. Must be the heat.

Violet stood up and excused herself, the others sat with their heads down, not saying a word. One of them looked up, offered a shrug. Violet nodded, then walked away.

There, Pram Boy, stay.
See your Mama
fatter about the face,
swollen-ankled, clomping of gait.
See she walks straight through
so that people move out of her way?

Yes, they see it now.

Stuck-up cow.

Not kneeling enough,
not preening or scraping on bended knee,
not bowing her head, not crossing herself.

Not crossing her legs, they say.

For your Mama, Pram Boy,
she is a rounded pod of seed
set to split like figs underfoot.

And like the figs grow bulbous on the trees
and the sellers sell their wares, or other things
And the men still thrust
and the murderers cut
and the thieves still rob
and the old still die
and the babies

Oh! the babies

they still cry,

So, Pram Boy, she carries on.

Come, come, Pram Boy,
pudding and pie,
Here's a story for boys who cry,
linger, digging in.

Like a foundling dumped in a hospital bin.

~

It was cooler back in the dormitory but it was too early to
go to bed. Violet listened to the swifts looping outside. A
fly buzzed at a windowpane.

She went to the washstand and splashed her face.
Maggie's bed stood empty to her right, the mosquito net
still tied in a knot.

Where was Maggie? Why didn't she come?

She walked over to Maggie's bed. It was made up the same as all the others, but there were no personal effects on display. No trinkets or notes from mother or sweetheart, no pressed flowers or cheap perfume. Only a hairbrush, her red lipstick and a book.

Violet took off the lid of the lipstick and wound it up. Its tip was slanted in a steep curve. Violet had watched her a thousand times: three quick strokes, smudged red lines.

She lay down on Maggie's bed. It was as if she had been cast adrift. She could no longer fathom how far she had come.

Far, far away from home. Now it was too late. She was too far gone.

Violet closed her eyes. The pillow was cool on her cheek. She sensed the beginnings of a dream, an in-between awareness of going home. Green moss, fetes with stalls of broad beans, radishes and peas.

She turned over and felt the weight of her belly drop, brought her leg up, settled her hip. Somewhere she was aware of the kicks and flips that would come and go each evening around this time.

She must have slept but it wasn't much later when she

stirred. She heard the door gently open and close.

Maggie was there.

Violet felt her sit down on the bed. She stroked her hair, said something so quietly that Violet couldn't hear. Then, as she half slept, she sensed Maggie loosening the net, pulling the mesh around them on the bed, lying down against Violet's back. She felt her sweep the hair away from her neck, then Maggie's warm breath, her lips, then her arm around her waist. Finally, she placed her hand on Violet's belly, on the firm, round flesh.

~

The next morning Violet made her way straight to her desk. One of the girls went round opening the windows and doors. The noise and smells from outside flooded in.

Violet settled herself in the hard metal chair and opened the first file.

Private Johnson, Robert. Born in Hull. A wife and three sons. Put forward for promotion in '43 but denied.

She flipped through the rest of the pile.

Private Higgins, James. Bristol, age nineteen.

Corporal Bennett, John. Somerset, six foot two.

The list went on. After a while it seemed pointless, men and boys all rolling into one. Violet stared out of the window to her right and tried to remember what it was like in Pontypridd last June.

Before any of this, she thought.

Before she even knew where Naples was. Before she signed up. When it was just her mother in the shop, the factory, Gwyn on her bike.

Before the autumn. Before the soldier arrived, standing in the kitchen. The way he smiled. The creases around his eyes. Their walks in the wood as the winter drew in.

Violet saw herself there without remembering what it was like. To be cold, to be all in a rush. She looked around the room at the few of them left, the sun bright behind the shades, the heat everywhere at once.

She turned to a new page in her logbook, entered the date at the top.

7th June, 1945.

She must be six months gone. She was round and downy and aglow. She was obscene, ridiculous. Everyone saw her, everyone must know.

Yet still, it felt like a gamble, what she was about to do.

Violet closed the files and lined up her pencil and pen to the side. She raised her hand to be excused and the Staff Sergeant nodded from her desk.

The Junior Commander's office was along the corridor on the left. Violet knocked. The clerk, an officer cadet with bad skin and greasy hair, looked at the floor.

After five minutes, the Commander called her in.

Violet stood staring into the middle distance somewhere above her head. The Commander replaced the lid on her pen. She looked calmly at Violet. They were silent for a long time. The Commander sighed.

Yes, Private?

Ma'am, I wish to report a concern that affects my work for the Corps.

Her work so far was without fault, the Commander said. Violet had the feeling that they were running through a script.

Thank you, Ma'am.

There was a pause.

Private, what is it you wish to say?

I'm pregnant, Ma'am.

The Commander nodded, resigned. Violet met her gaze straight on.

And you, Pram Boy?
You are a bullet
in the chamber of a gun,
The last one,
because this beautiful war is done.

~

Violet's processing out of the unit was swift. She told Maggie first and a couple of the others overheard. Some of the girls said they had known all along.

She packed her things and rolled up her cot the following morning. Only a couple of them stayed behind to say goodbye. Violet nodded and took their pats and well wishes, was quick to walk away and didn't look back.

Maggie was waiting and carried her bags. They walked along the same narrow streets, ragged clothes and faded bed sheets strung up above. Then the high-arched corridors of HQ, ready for transport to take her straight to the hospital.

Where she would stay. Where she would wait.

How far along? the Commander had asked the day before.

Violet watched her add it up and take out her file to check.

I see. This was before. So the father isn't in Italy?

Then she had pulled a blank memo onto the blotting pad on her desk.

You will have the baby here. I take it that is what you want?

They came to a stop at the bottom of the grand stone steps. Maggie put her bag down and gave her a playful salute. Violet was aware of the girls leaning at the balustrade above.

Then Maggie stepped forward and gave her a kiss on the cheek, said she would write. Violet must tell her when she could visit and she would come and take her out. Violet laughed out loud.

We'd make a right pair.

And Maggie gave her a flash of a look and walked on up the stairs.

PART FOUR

23

Naples laid itself out in the heat. Open drains, rotting meat. The city had lost its American dollars. Looting got worse, the people thinner, the Allied girls went back to their fathers and mothers.

The ATS ward was on the third floor and faced inwards to the hospital yard. The air sank with the indissoluble heat of July. When she arrived, Violet had been surprised to see other pregnant women pacing about slowly in the heat.

Yes, my dear, the Matron said. There are two kinds of patient here.

See, Pram Boy? Look what you have done.

And you are not the only one.

Oh ho! Did you think it?

No, alas.

Hundreds there are like you,
born bald and ugly and patched.

The women formed a slow-moving, ruddy group of their own, all of them further along than Violet was. They had their beds down one end while others came and went. Bouts of malaria, broken bones, or the pall and canker of one who'd lost an eye.

A couple of the others had smiled, gone over to introduce themselves. They asked how long she had left.

Three months, I think.

Until your confinement, one woman said. Then when the baby is a few weeks old they'll ship you home.

Like cargo, Violet joked.

They played bridge in the afternoons, were free to go for walks. The others talked of cramps or feeling their babies' kicks. Then the Matron would whip past them, check they'd made their beds.

They weren't sick, after all.

No. Most of them were just unlucky, caught in the riot and romance of the city. One of them had been in Rome but was transferred down. Only she among them had a sweetheart, an officer in the Italian Army. Her family knew but they wanted a marriage, she said. And so it was done, in the hospital chapel. The officer would visit occasionally and bring parcels of baby clothes, knitted or sewn by relatives and women from his village. The others would gather round her bed as soon as he left. They would hold up the little gowns and bloomers and smocks, tut with wonder, brush the soft fabrics close to their cheeks. Then gradually they would fall quiet, drift back to their beds.

The doctor came on the first afternoon. Violet wasn't sure if she had to salute. He told her to lie back on the bed and pressed her stomach with both hands.

Well. There's only one in there, that's good.

He pincered his grip at the base, pushing into her pelvis, her flesh, but grabbing at something else.

Baby is head down, he said.

She thought she felt him give it the slightest shake. She felt its feet in her ribs. The doctor returned her notes to the end of the bed and moved on to the next.

24

Violet and Flo sat at their usual table in the café down the road. Since the factory had been decommissioned Flo had got a job in the department store in town. There was a gentleman who came in twice a week, got her to try on costume jewellery for his wife, asked about her glove size, what time she finished work.

They ordered tea for two. Flo dangled her teaspoon into her cup. Violet didn't have much news.

Have you heard from Jack?

Flo shook her head. He'd broken it off last month. Redeployed, Violet couldn't remember where. He'd had a good war, was planning to stay on, had a good chance of a commission. Violet thought it was a bit of a shame. He was well-brought-up, always polite, not loud or too much in your way.

Well. Never mind. Probably for the best.

Yes.

Flo paused, put her teaspoon down.

Vi. There's something else.

Violet nodded, leaned closer across the tabletop.

I'm pregnant.

Oh!

Violet swallowed. She didn't know what to say. She took Flo's hand. Her parents knew, she said. And she'd told Jack, thought it would be all right.

As you say Vi, he was always polite.

A look. Violet winced.

But he'd hardly been in a rush to get down on one knee, she said. Then a week later he left. Posted to a depot near Crewe.

Crewe, that was it.

Flo pulled her hand away, turned her teacup round, lined the handle up with the spoon.

Oh Flo. What are you going to do?

Flo's voice was composed. Violet realised how carefully she must be choosing her words.

It was her mother who thought there might be a way.

Yes, Violet thought. That was how it would be. Her mother. She'd do anything for Flo. You could go over any time and she'd always be there, welcome you in. Chip pan on the stove and pots of pickles and jam, smelling of talc and sweat.

And it was a shame, they'd all liked Jack. But everyone knew how it went. Flo would go away for a while and her mother would take the baby when she came back. After all, she was the eldest of five, the youngest just turned six. What difference, really, if everyone thought her mother had one more than she really did?

They were silent, finally Violet looked up.

That baby's lucky, Flo.

Violet didn't add, So are you. She didn't need to, Flo knew.

25

Violet walked the corridors, faintly bored. The hospital was a world of its own. Entertainments, newsletters, radio. The closing of the German wing, the Polish ward. The visit of some dignitaries, the reduction of capacity to three hundred beds. Improvements to the cafeteria, the tennis courts, swimming trips on Wednesdays for the injured men.

Violet had written to Maggie and she'd written back. At first, she promised to come, then it was difficult, she said. She had engagements every weekend.

Engagements, Violet thought.

Or she hated hospitals, she said. Would rather write instead. She sent odd gifts – a rock of black pumice, a handkerchief trimmed with expensive lace. Then, despite herself, Violet began to watch for her approach, just in case. Saturday or Sunday afternoons, in the courtyard, or coming down the hall; she loitered or else shuffled back and forth.

After a while though, she gave up, found something else

to do. She took naps or sat propped up reading, tapping her fingers on her belly. She felt it morph and roll, go hard then soft.

The days dragged on. Soon, Violet was the only one left on the ward who wasn't ill. The last woman had gone into labour two days before. She went on for hours before they took her down, shouting for the midwife, then her mother, or just the pain. The same noises over and over again.

And your Mama, Pram Boy,
brought to the brink of rot
to the bough-break and canker-spot,
to the point of sweet juice
circled by wasps.

There she goes.

Wading through
the stinking heat
Lazy, they say, obese.
Chafing at the folds but bolder now,
letting everything hang out
Lolling about
like a sow with swollen teats,
like a cow beneath a shady tree
Clumped there, blank stare.

And the others, scratching at their stitches, looking on.

~

Violet slept lightly, woke often, groaned every time she turned. The church bells started every morning at six. She had taken to getting up and getting dressed, walking down to the piazza to watch the old women go to Mass. They were bent over and hunched, their black dresses dusty and creased, shuffling along in shoes that looked too big.

It was a Thursday morning and Violet waited in the shade on the other side of the square. The day was oppressively hot. She had a smock that she wore every day, it was already stained with sweat. She would rinse it out in the sink at night and hang it over the end of her bed.

The doors of the church opened and the women filed out. They shook holy water from their fingers and made the sign of the cross. Violet hung back until the last one of them had gone.

The church was cool and dark. She sat down in her usual place at the back. High on a plinth to her left was a statue of the Virgin Mary, rows of candles flickering at her feet.

Violet liked to look at her face. The pale skin was painted with circles of pink at the cheeks. Her lips were parted, her veil was white.

Violet looked down the length of the statue, at the bright blue plasterwork cloth draped over the small, flat breasts;

the knee protruding, the weight shifted onto the right hip. There was a green serpent trodden underfoot.

The gaudy colours shone. It bore no resemblance to the statues Violet was used to from home. All those mournful expressions, the pitiful stares. This one didn't seem to care. It certainly didn't demand that anyone kneel down to pray. It simply stood there, palms outwards, as if to say, Here I am.

Outside, the old women had pulled chairs into their doorways to sit until the sun came round. They pointed and smiled as Violet passed, talked to her as if she understood.

Si, si. Arriverderci, Signore.

She carried on. Past a bombed-out building that had only just collapsed, along the narrow street that led to the hospital gates.

On the ATS ward everyone was up, the nurses were doing their rounds. Sister Quinn nodded from the desk. Violet sat on her bed, out of breath.

After breakfast she might read her book.

Sleep.

Walk about, write a letter home.

Dear Mother, then some news. Most of it made up or half-remembered truths, or else general observations. Such as views of the sea from the port, the weather or the changing season.

Her mother's replies were forwarded from HQ and equally as bland. There were no more questions about when Violet was coming home, remarks about how they struggled without her help. Everything was contained and remote.

They bored her, and when she wrote again in reply, there was just a flattened, empty version of her life. No port, no cove, no filth, no decay. No light. No shade.

26

Violet stood waiting for the kettle to boil. Her mother opened the back door, swept the step, washed a mug in the sink and put the plates back in the cupboard from the rack.

VJ Day they were calling it. Victory over Japan. It was hardly a surprise after the bombs were dropped. Now the pictures were in all the papers again. Dirty great clouds of smoke. Photos from above showing everything flattened out. Then you'd look closely and notice the faint line of what used to be a road.

Why not celebrate? Her mother said. She ushered her to the table, told her to sit down.

All this about the atom bomb. The human race. It had nothing to do with them, everyone down here just trying to get on. Violet looked at the fried eggs on her plate, picked at the edge of one.

She was trying to lose some weight.

No, they were all just ants scurrying about, like those poor buggers in the ash. Still. They deserved it, the Japs. Everybody said.

Violet's mother fetched her tea and sat down. She nodded encouragingly as Violet picked up a piece of toast.

There. Fred'll be back soon, just you see.

Violet smiled, chewed drily on a crust.

Her mother was talking about plans for Fred's return. They could take a little break, she said. Then he ought to finish the house.

Violet nodded. Her mother went on.

Surely he'd be home on priority with the other married men?

Yes Ma. After they've sent the ones with children back first.

Her mother stood and wiped the table with the cloth.

Well. It won't be long, she said again, taking her apron off.

27

Maggie had sent Violet a note. She'd been demobbed that week and wanted to take her out. Violet thought about saying no but Maggie had told her the date and said she would come at twelve.

She was late.

Violet waited at the front of the hospital by the gates. Her eyes felt gritty and sore.

When Maggie came she was driving a motor car. She beeped the horn and the soldiers on guard motioned her past. The car was shiny black but had a dent in the side. She drove it in a tight circle, reversed to turn it round. Violet tried to be annoyed but Maggie squealed with delight.

Violet bent down to the window. The seats were a dark cherry red. She tutted, rolled her eyes.

Oh Violet, just get in!

She lowered herself down and Maggie nodded at her belly, impressed.

Well, Vi, I think everyone might guess.

She looked as dark and fine as she ever had, her long fingers resting on the steering wheel. She wore a black dress with wide straps that were slightly stiff, sitting proud of her collarbone.

Where are we going?

You'll see.

She wore her hair down. It blew wildly about her face as they drove along the high coastal roads. Maggie bellowed Violet's name like she had done on the boat.

The cove was already half in the shade. Maggie went ahead and paused at the rocky twist in the path, put out her hand for Violet to hold on to as she passed.

They set out their towels where they could lean their backs against a rock. Violet stretched her arms back, felt the space open up between her ribs. The sun warmed her face, her throat, her chest.

Maggie stepped around her like a nesting bird, picking this and that out of the bag.

Was this what their lives would be like, Violet thought, if they stayed?

They chatted about the people Maggie knew. Jeremiah had gone home two weeks ago. Nella was distraught, had taken to her bed. She was making plans to leave and go to Rome. Maggie tutted.

She ought to have known.

What about you? Violet asked. You're going home?

Maggie spat the seeds from a grape into her hand.

Well. She knew people in Switzerland. Also Paris, she said.

She unwrapped a fig from a crumpled bag. Some people she knew were heading north. She'd go with them as far as the border, then get across to Nice or Cannes.

She cut the fig into quarters, licked her fingers and the knife, offered Violet a slice.

No thanks.

Maggie paused, squinted in the light.

You could visit me, Vi. After it's born. When you're free.

Maggie. You think that's how it'll be?

Violet knew she sounded harsh, her laughter more of
a sneer.

Maybe for you, but not for me. *Free.*

She said it under her breath as if it was a curse. Maggie
didn't seem too concerned.

Well. Or we can write.

Violet sighed.

We can, Maggie, we can.

Then she heaved herself up, held on to the rock while she
kicked off her shoes.

Coming for a swim?

Violet waded in.

There she is, Pram Boy,
towering into the brine
With you inside,
>> *your tiny fingers*
>> *spread*
>>> *like suckers on glass,*
Stuck fast to her insides

As she dives
down into the bright bluegreen
and swims, your Mama,
Free now,
her belly down
among the polyp mouths of coral,
the beaking mouths of fish
pecking this way and that
For they know that you are in there,
amniotic in your sac.

The sea was silky warm. The white cotton of her underwear stuck to her skin. Violet stopped and tested the
depth, touched sand with the tips of her toes and closed
her eyes, bent her head back.

When Violet looked up again, Maggie was standing
naked on the shore. The high burn of the sun illuminated
her shoulders, the full weight of her breasts. There was
the jut of her hips, the dark 'v' of her pubic hair.

Violet stayed there treading water. It rose close to her
chin and she spat little mouthfuls out. She moved her
arms gently either side, watching all the time.

See that, Pram Boy?
Your Mama and her vision
of what you will become
You
and her lover's son,

Two sons
kissing like sailors out at sea
King-chested, mermen, tails entwined
Fork-tongued,
serpentine.

They swam for a long time.

~

They drove back in the calm of the late afternoon, the roads emerging round each bend and disappearing just as fast. The light was slanted with the end of summer. Maggie talked about her plans, the people she knew in France. Artists, émigrés, people who had fled during the war, fought in the resistance, been captured then escaped. Or Americans with interests overseas, reporters, mistresses of dignitaries.

People of independent means.

Maggie stopped the car just down from the hospital gates. She got out and walked around, opened the door and offered Violet her hand. They stood in the fading heat, the car clicking and creaking as it cooled.

Vi?

Yes.

Tell me, what are you going to do?

Violet sighed. Her skin felt like it was stretched taut across her face, her cheekbones high, her brow wide.

They'll send me home, Maggie. That's all I know.

I just think there are other places you could go. If you wanted to.

What, Maggie. Like you?

Violet picked up her bag, shifted her weight to the other foot. She knew what Maggie was trying to say, but now, finally, the refusal was hers to make. Perhaps she had been waiting all along. For the moment to bring it all crashing down. To show Maggie that she was wrong.

Because it was a ruse, a play. They were just the same as everyone else. Every other poor sod at the end of the war. They would all just go back to their rightful place.

It's not a game, Mags. There's nothing I can do.

She attempted a smile but Maggie caught her hand, pressed a piece of paper into her palm.

If you write – if you change your mind – they'll find me, wherever I am.

Violet looked down. Scrawled in pencil were two addresses. One was the British Embassy in Paris. Violet gave her a questioning look. Maggie shrugged.

And Violet knew, standing there in the dust, in the soft afternoon heat, that Maggie was a fantasy, a myth. Still, she stepped closer and took her face in both hands.

Maggie. With her delicate limbs, her lamblike bleating.

And she thought for a moment that she understood how it was. Men like Ted Barnes, Len Shale, how they wanted to possess women, still them with rough palms over their mouths.

But Maggie, this city, the baby, they were part of the same complex web. Violet had been caught, trapped. She was hollowed out.

No. They took too much, could not be kept.

When she looked back, Maggie was still there, leaning against the car. She held Violet's gaze, still with a direct stare, a smile that was a challenge, a dare. She had taken an orange from the bag. The peel spiralled brightly down from her hands as she broke it apart, put a segment in her mouth.

28

Violet walked and walked. Walked so that the cramps came, hitching up. Bitching at her lower back.

She walked across the courtyard. Men stared. As at a rare bud sprouting in the dust, or juicy apples, something moist and plump.

Violet let her cigarette end drop, trod it into the ground, stood watching people come and go.

Painfully slow.

She saw the injured transferred out, waiting for a convoy round the back. She watched as looters stole supplies, siphoned gasoline through a tube.

There were soldiers with their clothes pinned up around lost limbs, others with nervous tics. There were winks, double takes. A young man rubbed his crotch.

She moved on. Bad-tempered, swearing under her breath, wishing she had never done what she had done.

Smile! Might never happen, love.

Laughter.

Too late for that.

~

Later, Violet sat in a deep, tepid bath. She opened her eyes to stare at the ceiling above.

The baby inside was still.

She tapped her finger on the faint star of her navel.

There, and again there, that was it. A shift like a sigh across her belly. Jutting, cupped.

She pushed gently, felt the lamb-limb retract.

She stood up, muscle tight. Full at pelvis and ribs. She bent to hold the side, near-slipped as she climbed out onto the mat.

Looser again, she stood naked in the heat, dripping, strong. Then another thronged clenching, a hardening rise.

There.

Then gone; a breath.

She stretched her hands round the base of her back, licked her lips.

Looking down, she held her belly all veined, faintly mottled with red.

Come on now, let's be having you, she said.

29

Turn then, Pram Boy

Turn your sweet head.

As the afternoon falls quiet
in the dry September breeze;
            rustling,
            leaves

Turn,
swim down,
take your last amniotic sips

Before you're
                squirming
in the boundless air

        Nowhere

it will feel like,
        cold and shrill
        Until

you can cling to her flesh, both of you
inside out.

Hear her shout, Pram Boy?

There. So come.

Uterine-clencher.
Heart-wrencher.

Down through the heartbeat, down, down,
          and if your lungs fail
            there's purgatory waiting
               or else hell,

          so live!

Out then, come.

Yes.

There she is,
bent double
Now on her knees,
belly hard and
          slung beneath,
cervix
flattening,
a compression of herself
pushing at the fleshy mass

of you,

Out!

Come now, hush.
A moment's respite,
          release

Before your
un-knit skull
crowns
to the air

          To the burn of a ragged tear

And your Mama a cat
panting its
litter-runt
free

And you are caught there

before,

there there,

you are limb-free and lung-kicked
                              into the air!

155

                    Oh! flailer boy,
                    vernix-smeared and purplish
                    Chest
        concave
                    for breath

Slapped to a wail,
                    crying,
                            held aloft.

Oh!

There.

Breathe, Pram Boy, hush.

Mother-lover,
Mother
Son.

Now, the
hunger has begun.

Now the pulsing cord is cut,
knotted off

And you,
Behold your true mother-love

Already not enough.

So move!

Move your tender snap-neck,
your sucking mouth,
all needs now outside yourself.
Grubbing about for food,
head bouncing,
seeking a tongue-click latch
to work the glands beneath the flesh
Nose wet like a cub

And she is sweet and salty with sweat
and metallic with blood.

And you?

                     You are pinking up.

There. Find her, then.

Press
        your face, fill
your mouth
        with her flesh
pressed
        into your working jaw,
your sucking tongue,
Lungs quivering wetly in your ribs,
        nostril flare.

There.

Open your eyes, she says.

Yes, you.

See her float at the edges of your field,
your heartbeat stilled,
you are wrapped and warm.

And for your Mama,
a blood-pour,
the sweat not yet dried in her matted hair,
blood not yet stemmed
and there is   piss and shit pooled on the floor,
blood in the towels and
warm water bowls

All to be swilled away.

But not you.

Look how she holds you.

Look!

How you keep to her,
there now, hold it in,
          A feeling,
damply slipping away,

the memory of her milky skin,
your claw at her breast.

Remember.

Remember this.

And everything now in sharp relief,
clear and cold as a glass-edge.

Focus your eyes, find her gaze.

There.

You meet again.

30

A boy.

Better that way, she heard someone say.

Then the baby was wrapped up tightly and taken away.

She strained to hear him cry in another room.

~

Soon, where the blood had flowed they were mopping up.

Her own flesh was swabbed and stitched and she winced with pain but did not cry out, instead tried to listen, stay alert.

He was brought to her again. The midwife came, her breasts were adjusted and handled, the milk manipulated from her nipples, his head shoved about.

~

For three days in a separate room there seemed only flesh, soilings, milk. A recurring tide that took her in and out of sleep. Split nipples, nipples that cracked and bled, red-orange and erect, flat to a gummy gnaw, her stomach an empty sack.

And she bled from inside and from other cuts; knuckles raw from wringing out wet cloth and other places torn, swollen out of shape. Agape, like a schoolboy's joke.

She moved slowly about; small steps around the bed, crouching on the pot, pissing messily, gritting her teeth until the stinging stopped.

And yet. When she saw him she would forget. They were sea creatures in the deep. Tendrils and fingers and suckers and limbs. When they were pulled apart she clung on, rushed back, became entangled again.

~

Back on the ward, the nurses came clattering on their daily rounds.

Her milk flowed. It seemed to engulf them both, spurted and missed his mouth. They were frantic and maddening, the baby blindly gasping.

Or else she held him, piss-wet, the liquid warm against his skin. And she laid him out on the bed, his penis pissing in an arc again; bathed his navel where the two of them had once been joined; cleaned the folds of his groin of yellow shit; felt the thin membrane of his scrotum drag; tipped his head back, wiped the milk-sick from the creases of his neck.

~

At night he suckled in the dim pool of the bedside lamp. After, she held his lolling head in her hands.

His hot cheeks, his pink mouth.

And she peeled his fingers from his palm, felt the sharpness of his tiny fishbone nails; watched his chest for signs that his lungs inhaled, breathed breaths. His mouth was a bow to the arrow of his tiny tongue that popped out, or lay flat in his mouth when he wailed.

And his toes, all ten.

And his softly rounded head.

And his ears, nose, eyes with their lashes growing in.

She could not believe him, could not take him in.

PART FIVE

31

The city yawned and cracked its bones, a giant waking from sleep.

Bomb sites where boys jeered and goaded dogs with sticks were cleared. Nettles and dock leaves, steel and coal. Prefabs sprang up with concrete slabs for walls and thin wooden doors.

Families moved in and out. No Irish, no blacks. Tradesman's entrance round the back. People saved scraps and boiled bones like before, ate offal or the tail end of things, mended, repaired.

Men came home from the war, some rich, some poor. VD, the clap, worse things were gone, some were fit to work but there were some who couldn't get it up because the war was done.

And the women were beaten, or adored. Slack-wombed, baby-boomed. Deflowered or else not getting enough. Or getting too much, that one. Wayward daughters, wandering-eyed, were chastised, their mothers nagging on and on.

What's wrong with you, woman?

Back in the house, in the kitchen, in the bedroom lying there not saying a word. And in the morning, washing the sheets of beer-piss and come, down on their knees, the stains all stripped and scrubbed and bleached.

Then they made their beds, these women. Shifted shape, got on.

~

The last Violet heard, Fred was in France. Everyone else was already home. Frank and Bill, Tommy Knock. People had stopped asking about Fred, must be wondering where he was.

To get that far had taken four months, from Rangoon to Calcutta, across India then up through the Suez Canal. And now the winter had settled in. The veg patch was crisp with frost. Violet stood at the sink and watched a magpie hop from light to shade across the yard.

The letter had come last Friday, from Marseilles. She'd waited for him at the station every day since then. She'd cleaned the house, got some of his things back out. His winter hat and coat, the ashtray by the chair. They were all sitting there, gathering dust.

Violet finished the washing-up and dried her hands, then fixed her hair in the hall mirror. She looked at her watch.

If she left now she'd be in time for the twelve o'clock.

See her, Pram Boy, for you did not know her then.
Strong arms, jaw set,
in the kitchen over suet
and pickles and pastry edges.

Rationed on the dregs,
powdered milk and eggs.

Wait then, Pram Boy.
Then wait some more.

Pinny-frill, milk spill, knock on the door.

Wait like she is waiting
for your daddy,
gone to war.

Will he come, your daddy,
a soldier clean and new?
Grinning like a boy
made to love a boy like you.

Violet pulled the front door shut. Her breath misted the air. She turned the corner, past her mother's. Mrs Grey from number twenty-two came out.

Violet mouthed that she couldn't stop.

Off to wait for Fred.

Any day now, the neighbour said, and they'd all be glad to see him home and do send him round to say hello.

That's right, Violet thought, they'd all want to see Fred. With his wavy hair and strong arms, whistling through the gap between his teeth.

After the miscarriage, and everything taken out, some of the girls had asked Violet what she was going to do. She never quite knew what to say. Of all the girls from the factory she was the only one. Married, keeping house. There was Elizabeth but that was hardly going well. They lived with Tony's sister and mother in a tenement flat. His family spoke Italian all the time. She held little hope of liking the food they cooked, she wrote, and they still hadn't been to New York.

Then there was Flo, hiding away in Worcester at her aunt's.

No, she was lucky, she thought.

She'd reached the tram stop outside Norton's Department Store. It didn't take long until Violet got off in the centre of town and walked the rest of the way. At the station she stood in her usual spot and watched. You had to look for the khaki caps. The soldiers always sidled off in twos or threes. Shifty-looking, ill at ease.

The stationmaster caught her eye. Violet smiled, rubbed her hands together to lament the cold. He nodded, stamped his feet.

Nice-looking, Violet thought. Always neat. Probably on a decent wage.

The train came to a slow stop. Violet waited for everyone to get off, stood on tiptoes to scan the crowd. There were a few stragglers, a soldier strolling off with his girl. She was all pink and smudged, he'd knocked her hat askew. He kept squeezing her shoulders, pulling her close to his side, almost tripping her up each time.

Violet turned, the low sun in her eyes.

No Fred today. She was suddenly anxious to get home. She smiled again at the stationmaster and he tipped his hat. Outside she looked right then left before crossing the road.

On the other side was a familiar silhouette.

Sitting on a bench, leaning forward smoking a cigarette, was Fred.

Look, Pram Boy.

There they are.

How she catches her breath, shallow in her chest
The way he   turns his head,
stands up, grins,
            flicks away his cigarette.

Yes, that's them.
Catch them if you can,

down the Arms for a drink,
at the piano with a carnation in her hair
Or laughing with his head thrown back,
pint in hand,
            a flash
            of the gap
between his two front teeth,
his olive skin,
his hair a lighter shade of brown than before.

Handsome, like he'd won the war.

So tap the window with your tiny claw, peer in
Later, when they are grasping at the evening's ends
            See how they linger in each room of the house,
picking things up, putting them down
            Sitting down and standing up,
laughing, embracing
            Dancing a little; a little drunk.

Yes. There they are.

It is late when they grow still,
standing in the front room
with the deep chill of the night coming on,
their bodies warm, pressed close,
as they reach their hands up to undo each other's clothes.

~

It had snowed overnight and the light when they awoke was a flat, telltale grey. Violet sat up in bed, listening to Fred down in the kitchen putting the kettle on the stove. She felt the draught and knew he had left the back door open, having a smoke.

Fred? She called. No reply.

By the time she got down, Fred was already outside. She went to the front window to look. The snow was blocking doorways in drifts all the way up the street. Fred was busy clearing a path, he didn't stop. He bent over in a steady rhythm cutting great blocks of snow, twisting his torso to throw them into the road.

Violet thought back to the year before. Nearly Christmas, still the war. She'd have been wondering by now if they'd had some luck, if something had stuck.

Embryo. Funny word. No way to know, back then, that there were two. Or that she'd lose them soon.

She knocked on the window. Fred turned and she pointed

up the road. The boys from number eighteen had come out. Father killed in France, mother a nurse. You often saw them, hanging about. They were all bundled up in wool, the smaller one holding the big one's hand.

They called to Fred, packing great balls of snow in their hands. He pretended not to hear, then rounded on them, giving chase, nearly falling over himself. They threw their snowballs and missed, Fred made roaring sounds and when he caught them, they pulled him down to the ground.

After about half an hour he came in. He was out of breath, stamping his boots. Violet tutted at the snow melting on the mat.

Fred grinned, rolled another cigarette.

Funny, when he was away she'd almost forgotten how he was, had worried that they wouldn't have anything to say.

After their quick goodbye, him walking away past the bins.

Twins, the doctor had said.

But they'd already gone by then. Scraped out. A surprise that came too late. They would have shaken their heads, said things like, Twins, imagine that!

Fred had finished his cigarette and was taking off his boots. Violet moved them onto the newspaper she'd put down.

Vi? he said.

Yes?

I thought now I'm back we could write to enquire.

About what?

Violet could feel him watching her as she laid the table with knives and forks, two mats.

About a baby. A little boy.

Adoption, he said. He had it all planned out. They'd tell him, of course, when he was old enough to understand. They'd say he was chosen. They'd put it like that.

Chosen. Violet nodded. A baby boy. They'd tell him that they chose him. Perhaps that would be enough.

Of course it would, said Fred. He'd be our son.

32

The boy was three months old. His eyes were alert to her smile, his head turned to the sound of her voice. His mouth moved at her breast, his sweet breath, his long fingers grasped hers, clutched at her flesh, let go, clutched again. His feet were always cold, his legs long and thin, dangling loosely when she held him and he slept, a soft, heavy weight.

She had brought him back. To England in December, standing on the scrubby tarmac in the cold, waiting for the Duty Officer to come. In an ill-fitting uniform, with a baby crying in her arms, she'd stood with his papers in her hand, flicked-through, signed and rubber-stamped.

Living Male Child, born 03:15, 15th Sept, 1945.

And under *Name and Nationality of Father*, and *Rank*,

~   ~

Two tildes. Two columns, blank.

Now every day was the same. The ATS Special Discharge

Depot was on the outskirts of Birmingham, the barracks home to an infantry battalion and a military prison.

She had twenty-eight days, the sergeant said when she arrived. Enough time to sort your affairs and go home.

At least she had her own room. There was a cradle for the baby that they had borrowed from an officer's wife, a chest of drawers, a sink, a shelf and a single bed. On the first night she had dreamt of tiny baby birds, grubby and taut-necked. Then of Maggie crossing an English lawn, pregnant and wearing a black dress.

Not waving but drowning, Maggie in the dream had said.

And Violet was holding back her hair to better see her face, then her hands were round her waist.

Sometimes, she was tempted to write, but what was the point?

~

She awoke with a headache as usual. The baby was crying. The nights were still fretted with his noise. Trappings and exhalations of air, cold fingers and toes, hawklike arcs of hunger cried out every three or four hours. Then he would wheeze, Violet would jolt up to look, then he would seem not to be breathing at all.

She took him into bed with her and fed him again. It was

six in the morning and pitch-black. Outside, she could hear the barracks coming to life, vehicles turning, still needing their headlights. When the baby had finished, falling asleep with his mouth slack, a trickle of milk coming out, she left him on the bed and lit a cigarette.

She stood at the window and inhaled in quick, sharp breaths. Some soldiers were gathering on the parade ground below, blowing into their cupped hands, smoking or scuffing the ground. Violet rubbed the sleep out of her eyes and wiped her nose on the back of her hand. There was ice on the inside of the windowpanes.

The soldiers were lined up in squadrons ready to march in basic formation. Violet stubbed out her cigarette. There were always a few of them out of step.

She'd been excused from drill herself, as well as exercise and inspection. The other women eyed her suspiciously every morning in the breakfast room. They'd be making their tea and toast as Violet boiled water for teats, tested droplets of milk.

The baby was awake and grizzling. She watched him from above. His nose was glistening with snot, his cheeks were red and cracked with cold.

His mouth, his lips, his tongue. The fleshy ridge of his gums. It seemed to Violet that he would consume the world if he could, take the slippery solidity of everything into his mouth. He sucked his fist raw and her nipples huge and flat, left trails of spit on her shoulders or mouth marks of wet cloth.

In Naples, he had lain bare-limbed like a grub getting fat. When he was not taken away to sleep in a tight cocoon of cloth, she would hold him lolling at her chest. Now he lay in layers of cotton and wool that forced his arms into stiff, padded slugs at his sides.

He cried and cried.

~

It was two weeks before Violet could get home. The sergeant gave her leave and a girl called Rose agreed to have the baby in her room overnight. Violet left his bottle and clothes along with a note. His papers were in the drawer, she said.

Make sure you come back, the girl joked.

It took the whole day to get to Pontypridd by train. When Violet finally arrived, she walked straight past her mother's shop.

She needed more time, didn't want to look.

As she walked, she imagined turning up with the baby in her arms.

Yes, she would say. The one I gave birth to while I was away.

She stopped at the bridge and took a deep breath. The water below was brown, the banks tangled and steep. She looked at the gentle hills ahead, patched with fields, the woods darkly green. She thought how grey everything had been since she got back. Birmingham, the parade ground. Clanking flagpoles instead of trees. Bare, flat brick.

She closed her eyes, opened them again.

It felt good to be home.

She picked up her bag and walked back up the street. It was Saturday closing time and the shops were all winding their awnings in. The haberdashery was about halfway up on the left. Violet stood outside, looking in. The black-out blinds had gone and the electric lights glowed. There was a Christmas garland of holly hung up with ribbon in the window.

That would be Aggie, Violet thought.

She had forgotten how handsome it all was. The polished oak, the glass cabinets and lamps hanging low over the bank of drawers.

And there was her mother. She was standing on a stool with her back turned. She looked smaller, a little hunched.

Violet ducked to the side. The butcher opposite saw her and gave a wave from behind his counter. She nodded and smiled, turned round, opened the door.

Her mother gave a short gasp.

Violet grinned, went over and leaned up to kiss her cheek.

For a moment they didn't know what to say, how to speak.

Her mother climbed down, leaning on Violet's arm.

So! You came back.

She pointed to the yarn she wanted bringing down. Violet took off her coat and reached up to the shelf. She felt her mother's eyes on her back.

Well. You've filled out.

Violet rolled her eyes.

Yes, Ma, I'm all grown up.

There was a pause. Violet waited in case there was something else her mother wanted to say. Her hair had turned grey at the temples and in a streak at the front. Her curls were severe, set tight to her head. But there was something about her that looked frail, like it might crumble and give way.

Aggie will be back soon. She's run up to the bank. I've got used to having her about.

That's good, Ma. I'm glad.

And Violet walked round the counter and through to the house.

~

When Aggie got back her mother went out to catch the butcher before he closed. Aggie saw Violet and gave a gleeful shout, unravelling her long scarf from her neck, her cheeks picture-book red.

At dinner, her questions bubbled around the room. The weather in Italy, the Royal Palace, the Duomo, the food. All that Violet had written about before.

She wanted to hear it again, she said, first-hand.

Then her mother asked what were her plans. What about Christmas? What about coming back, settling down?

It's redeployment, Ma. Just a few more months.

She said nothing, sat still as stone.

Was it voluntary? she wanted to know.

It was easier by letter, Violet thought. Now, sitting in the kitchen with the sound of the clock, there was nothing to say that wasn't made up.

Aggie ushered the conversation on. The shop, the town, sons who hadn't come back from the war.

What about that Polish boy, did you hear from him, Vi?

Violet's mother appeared not to have heard, stood up and turned to the sink. Crockery knocked together in the water as she washed a cup.

I've no idea, Aggie. He'll be far away, no doubt.

~

Upstairs, Violet undressed and got into bed. She felt the ache of a missed feed in her right breast. After a while she heard her mother come up. There was the opening of a drawer, the knock of hangers in the wardrobe as it creaked shut. Then quiet, before the murmur of her voice, a steady drone.

She would be kneeling at her bed, hands clasped in prayer, head down.

Violet turned off the lamp and let her eyes adjust to the familiar shadows of her room.

Naples felt so far away. The dirty yellow streets, the American jeeps and motorcycles, the veg stalls, the dark-haired young girls. She had watched them all recede from the back of the truck as it drove away, the baby sleeping on her lap. Then a few factories flattened by bombs as the city fell off into farmland, red earth churned to mud by the cold rain that had come.

Compared to Wales, it was still warm.

She remembered the airmen had shown her how to strap the baby to her chest, handing her various bits of meshing and clips.

And she had thought, they would have seen bloodier, leakier cargo than this.

Then the plane, sitting straight-backed in the endless din, the thin scar of her perineum throbbing anew, until they landed into sleet and snow.

Violet plumped her pillow under her neck. The boy would be sleeping now, tucked up in his barrack room cot. The grey, chipped walls. The flickering light over the sink. She worried that he'd be too cold, hadn't had enough milk.

She tried to imagine him close to her now. The gentle rise and fall of his chest as she watched him sleep, the occasional flutter of breath, his head turned to one side. Or tiny clothes in the chest of drawers, some toys on the mat. Or even with her mother in the shop, batting about the spools of thread.

She saw him in short trousers, woolly hat; a good trapper in the woods, mud trowelled on the edge of his boots.

In the bath she would scrub him with her sleeves rolled up, arm grabbed, wriggling like a worm on a hook.

Imagine that, Violet thought. Like a story in a book.

She turned over in bed, drifted off, but it wasn't long before she was woken up. Her nightdress was wet with milk and clinging to her breast. She sat up and propped the pillow behind her back, picked up the glass from her bedside table. Holding it on her lap, she leaned over and squeezed her nipple until it was beaded with drops.

She tried to imitate the regularity of his sucks. Now the milk came in creamy, thicker drops. It trickled through her fingers as she squeezed the nipple flat. She leaned further over the glass.

33

Violet picked her way through the potholes and gravel of the haulage yard, looking for Fred among the trucks.

The dog pulled at its chain and barked at her, rattling the fence. She made her way to the cabin and placed Fred's lunch tin on the shelf.

She stood for a moment watching the men at a fire burning in an old oil drum. They were sallow-skinned and listless. Out of work, most of them. They turned up hoping for a few hours' pay, drawing on family connections, the Irish, or else they were sent there by people who knew Fred would help.

Violet looked around her. Fred's overalls on a hook, papers stuffed in bulldog clips, an empty tea-stained cup. All of it thumbed with engine oil.

There was nothing here of the factory where she and the girls had worked. No one took care of themselves or polished their boots.

No, this was no place for a woman.

Fred had joined some of the men by the fire. They smiled warily, laughed at his jokes. He'd taken the business over from her father as soon as he got back. He never spoke about Burma and she didn't like to ask.

All in the past.

Earlier in the war he'd brought her souvenirs or gifts. She had a bracelet from the Gold Coast, hammered out in silver by a boy in the camp. It was a chain of plates and links, with her initials and his regimental crest. But the clasp was rough and caught on her clothes. It didn't look like anything that Flo or Elizabeth might wear. She kept it on the dresser but it tarnished, so she put it in a drawer.

Fred had gone back to work, rubbing his palms, slapping the men's backs, shaking their hands until they dispersed.

Violet shivered. She hated the yard.

She decided to carry straight on, slipped round the gate brushing the hem of her coat and straightening her hat. She was on her way to visit Flo, who'd returned from Worcester two days ago. She'd sent a note for Violet to come round.

~

Flo was in the back room with the baby on her lap. It was only a few weeks old.

Oh, Flo. She's a bonny little thing.

Violet crouched down and squeezed the baby's feet in her hands, bicycling her legs, kissing her toes. A girl all in frills. June was her name.

Flo's mother came in. Her sister Eleanor was there too. Eleanor picked the baby up and kissed her, squeaking loudly at her cheek. Her mother peered in close and tucked a frill under her chin. They made cooing noises as they carried her out to another room.

Flo exhaled loudly, flopped back in her chair. She spoke in detail of the birth, how long it had gone on.

She had been sick as a dog, she said. And the burning sensation when the head was there; how she thought she actually heard it go, the tear.

Never again, Vi, I swear!

She was still talking about the birth when Eleanor came back with June in the crook of her arm. Violet stood up, made clicking noises with her mouth. June's eyes tried to focus at the sound.

Would you like a hold, Vi?

She was so light. Her head lolled slightly as Eleanor handed her across. She writhed a little, took a shuddering breath. Violet started bouncing left to right. Then they all stood there for a while, Flo and Eleanor smiling at June in her arms, their heads on the side.

She loves that, Vi.

Yes, it was good to see Flo. She always sailed through. As if difficult things were boring. As if there were better things to do.

She was talking about her plans, about going back to her job in town. The business with the baby had been hushed up enough so they'd agreed to take her back on. She and Eleanor would share a room, she said, and June would sleep in their mother's bed.

And that was how it went, Violet thought. People adapted, moved on. Especially Flo. And June would never need to know.

Vi, shall we go to the caff before you have to get back?

The baby had fallen asleep in Violet's arms. Flo took her and with her free hand picked up her coat.

Come on, I'll hand her over to Ma and we can go.

And how they will watch you grow, these women.
Hawkish, pinching your cheeks between forefinger and thumb,
knowing all along, Pram Boy,

whose children belong to whom
Whose are the mothers, daughters, sisters, aunts,
relationships all fluid and undone.

See your mother among them,
she can play any tune you'd care to name
Good seamstress, excellent cook,
will patch you up
at elbows and knees,
sew tiny coal sacks for your Dinky trucks,
which you will empty in her shoes
squirming out of her grip.

Little shit.

Never aware, Pram Boy
of how everything
must be repaired,
reused;
might be lost

Until you will say it yourself one day:

You are not my mother,
        you are not.

34

The Adoption Society's imperative, the nun said, was to make permanent and secure arrangements for the child's moral and physical health.

The office was down some steps at the end of the hall. The house would once have been grand but now the paint on the walls was chipped and the tiles on the floor were cracked. Violet could hear the sound of plates being stacked in the scullery next door.

She sat calmly, her suitcase at her feet and her coat on her lap. The baby had been taken by a young nun at the door. The Mother Superior was poised with a pen in her hand.

The Order of the Sisters of St Paul ran the mother and baby home. Adoptions were arranged by Father Hudson's Homes.

Violet had written to an administrator called Father William McBride. The reply had come straight away.

Boys were hard to place, he said. Could she not make arrangements with her diocese in Wales? Would her mother not take the baby in her place?

Violet wrote again and he promised to make enquiries on her behalf. It was another week before she heard. The NCO at the depot said something about bleeding hearts, taking in waifs and strays. Then she signed the papers and Violet was discharged. She was given ration coupons, a train warrant and a change of civilian clothes.

The nun picked up two forms from a pile in a tray. Babies went to good Catholic families, she said. Mothers were offered temporary lodgings nearby and permitted to visit once a day.

Until such time . . .

Violet shifted under her gaze.

You say the boy was baptised?

The nun licked her finger and thumb, flicked through the papers Violet had brought. Her desk was flanked by a statue of the Virgin Mary and a painting of the conversion of Saul.

Through the window behind her, Violet could see a garden with raised beds and the purplish leaves of winter veg poking raggedly out of the soil.

She thought of the day in Naples when she had carried him down. Out of the ward, across chequered floors, through the hospital yard shielding him from the sun. To the chapel with its wooden pews and cool white walls.

He was three weeks old. In the morning she had given him a bath then dressed him in a white gown handed down by one of the girls. It had an embroidered collar and tiny pearl buttons at the back.

The nun put her glasses on and held the papers up to the light.

Baptised by US Army Chaplain, Father Victor L. Dux?

Yes. Violet had been to see the priest before the baby was born. He invited her to sit down, nodded as she spoke. Then he'd asked if she wanted to go to confession and Violet had said no.

Right. Shall we get on?

The nun picked up a form and pressed down hard with her pen.

Mother?

Violet stated her name and date of birth.

Father?

There was a pause, then Violet spoke.

Len Shale.

Pontypridd, Wales.

Age 24.

The nun finished the forms and stamped each one.

Violet waited while the nun bustled about, went to the filing cabinet, sat back down. And she thought about the Polish soldier on the train to Aberdeen, his delicate hands clean-scrubbed, his hair parted on the side, going back to his sweetheart or his bride, for all she knew.

For all she knew.

But it was too late. It was done.

The nun tore off the top copy of the form, clipped it together with the papers on the desk.

And it wasn't about blame, or naming names. Or even erasing the soldier from her past. It was just about moving on.

A fresh start. And now the boy was British born.

After they'd finished with the forms, the Mother Superior led her back along the hall. Sounds of wails and voices came from somewhere behind a door. Another nun came out.

Don't worry, he's settled down.

Sister Cathy was her name. She was tall and thin with a gentle voice, the crushed t's of an Irish accent mixed with something else. Wisps of pale hair had come free from the tight white band around her face. Her wimple wasn't quite straight and her cheeks were pink. She had pushed the sleeves of her habit up and rolled the white cuffs of her blouse back over the top.

She opened the nursery door.

There was noise as well as light. There were bangs and cries and jangling toys. Someone was singing a song.

The boy was lying on a rug and a nun sat grasping his hands, clapping them together in limp little fists.

The nursery was where they played in the day, Sister Cathy said. Next door was where they slept. They went through to the adjoining room where the blinds were drawn. There were four cots. Two babies were asleep in one.

In the corner sat an old pram.

PART SIX

35

All that spring, Violet and Fred worked on the house. They worked on their hands and knees, up ladders to clean or paint or hammer in nails. They hung pictures, waxed drawers, sanded down then varnished doors.

Daffodils and hyacinths came out again, sickly scented in the yard every time they brushed past. Children loitered in the street out front, kicked balls and played with splintered wood, metal sharpened to a point, makeshift carts and prams, dirty hands.

When Fred wrote the letter, he asked for a boy. It was a week later when they received a reply.

I am delighted to know that you wish to adopt a little baby boy, and I feel sure we shall be able to find one suitable for you.

The letter was signed Father William McBride. They were to send their marriage certificate and fill in the enclosed medical form. A health visitor would call round to inspect their home.

How would they manage? Violet thought.

She had measured up for curtains in the back room. Her mother had some fabric spare. It was pale yellow with green sprigs. Violet went up to check one more time. She opened the door, stepped into the light.

Hello? she said.

It echoed.

Violet remembered when they had painted the room white. So pleased with themselves, their little wedding and the house. Just a few days, going to bed in the afternoons, knowing that Fred would go away again soon.

And oh, they had been full of plans.

She went to the window. Fred was digging over the raised beds out back. He had taken his shirt off and hung it on the fence, stripped down to his vest. Violet watched as he laid down a plank, bent down, made a furrow in the soil with his hand.

He saw her at the window and waved. Then he held out his palm for her to see the tiny seeds.

She shook her head, frowned.

Summer carrots! he mouthed.

There.

Clutch her hand, Pram Boy
as she stands in the room at the top of the house
painted white and clean and ready.

Ready for who?

Ready for you.

Or see her face
covered in cold cream at night,
her bedjacket tight
under her chin,
haunted
by the idea that you exist, somewhere.
A boy like you,
blond-curled
good as new.
Perhaps a little thin,
wearing
borrowed clothes
         with holes in.

Knock knock, who's that?

Oh for you have your bags packed, Pram Boy,
waiting by the door.

Stork-dropped, listening
eager for more.

36

The priest had put out for a housekeeper soon after Violet arrived. The presbytery was on the other side of the church. Sister Cathy had suggested she apply and she'd been working there six days a week, paying upkeep for the boy. She visited each day, went round the back way and let herself in, helped with lunch sometimes, got him up from his nap, gave him his bottle, sang to him on her lap.

And he grew like an apple on a tree, sat and played with a spinning top, clapped his hands. He was eight months old, already crawling round, wide-eyed and bold.

She did the ironing in the afternoons when the kitchen got the sun. There were three sets of linen for Mass. She sprinkled each cloth with water, pressed down hard then flipped them over in half. She put the linens in the basket and quickly finished the rest. A shirt, three hankies, a tea towel, two vests.

She heard the front door slam shut.

All right, Violet?

The priest was a short, fat, unkempt man. Father John. He was from Liverpool and Violet liked the way he spoke. Lazily almost, with a sardonic drawl. She cooked him breakfast every day, then they would go across to the church in time for early Mass.

The priest wandered through to the kitchen, his collar unclipped, scratching his chest. His hair stuck out in tufts from his head. He spoke through the cigarette in his mouth.

You off soon, Violet?

Yep.

She indicated his supper plated up and covered on the stove.

Righto.

He'd never said anything, Father John. Never asked about her past. He knew about the boy, would ask her how he was. And she would mention little things: the time he nearly choked on a wooden bead, the other day when he was stung by a wasp.

Violet went through to the hall and put on her coat, checked herself in the mirror, picked up her keys and called goodbye.

Father John popped his head round the kitchen door.

God bless, Vi.

37

The man from the Public Health Department sat on the settee, a cup and saucer in one hand and his briefcase on his knee.

A formality, he said.

Violet smiled.

He put the cup and saucer on the table she had placed at his side.

He had some questions he must ask, if they didn't mind?

Fred stood by the window. She wished he would sit down. Violet glanced around the room one final time.

She'd worked solidly for two weeks. Blacked the hearth and grate, and the stovetop, and beaten all the rugs. Even scrubbed the flags out in the yard. She had finished the curtains for the back bedroom and put a chair in there, and a chest, which was empty except for a blanket and some sheets.

Because what could they get for a child who would arrive, just like that?

And for Violet, no waiting, no nine months.

No doctors, no midwives. No carrying high or low. No one for sorrow, two for joy, three for a girl, four for a boy. No old wives' tales, no health advice. No cravings, no Guinness for iron. Nobody giving up seats on the bus. No bed rest, no labour, no birth.

38

Violet took the path round the back of the church, up through the garden past the vegetable patch. She'd helped get some of the early crops in. Now it was a riot of bright green. The nuns who worked in the kitchen saw her coming and let her in.

She was in time to get the boy up from his nap. Sister Cathy was sitting reading a book.

He's all yours, she said.

It was her little joke. Only once, she had hinted at something else.

Violet, you could keep him, you know?

She had been watching as Violet gave him a bath, soaped his arms, squelched her hand in between his legs, cleaned between his fingers and toes. Sister Cathy had taken the jug and doused his hair. The boy's eyes closed and he gasped, laughed; so did they.

Violet had lifted him onto the towel on her lap and

wrapped him tightly as he sucked his thumb. And Sister Cathy had asked her why she couldn't take him home.

She had listened calmly to Violet's reply. The town, her mother, the rest of her life stretching ahead. And then Sister Cathy had told her that she was wrong. That Violet was strong, that God would forgive.

Violet shrugged. That's the thing. I don't think of him as a sin.

Sister Cathy bent to pick the towel up from the floor. Violet tried to soften her tone as she gathered up the boy's clothes. He deserved more, she said. Didn't ask to be born.

Isn't that what everybody thinks?

Sister Cathy's face was set in a passive smile.

Yes, I suppose it is.

Violet went back to combing his hair. They hadn't spoken about it since.

~

She opened the nursery door a crack. All the other children were asleep in the row of cots but the boy would only sleep in the broken pram, jammed into the corner behind the door. It was grand and deep and its springs creaked.

The flat base of its bed was long gone. He was curled up on a pile of blankets, sucking his thumb.

Only one other child was awake but she hadn't made a sound. She had brown skin with soft, curly hair and dark eyes. Her nose ran constantly. Violet rarely heard her cry. When Violet asked, the nuns would shake their heads. Nobody would take her, they said.

Violet picked up the boy. His hair was damp with sleep, his neck smelled biscuity and clean. He sighed and leaned his head on her shoulder, put his thumb back in.

He was doted on, she knew. Everybody said. His eyes were pale blue and there were blond little curls forming at the back of his head.

That boy, Sister Cathy would say. Nothing will stand in his way.

Violet knelt down with him on the rug next door. He was learning to stand with hands held, then would wobble and fall. He clutched at her blouse, butted her with his head. Still, sometimes, he would try to shuffle down to her breast.

Violet, will you give us a hand?

Sister Cathy was getting the others up. Violet put the boy down. He howled, his face turned bright red. She made a smacking noise with her mouth.

Now now, I'm coming back.

One of the cots was wet. Violet got fresh sheets while Sister Cathy tended to the babies crying for milk. She moved quickly, stripped the cot, flipped the mattress, smoothed it flat.

The boy was crying furiously in the other room. Violet finished the cot and went to pick him up. She kissed him, looked into his watery eyes.

Hush now, Mama's here.

He gave a final cry, was calm. Then he grinned and bounced a little in her arms.

39

Fred opened the letter and read it out loud.

Would they kindly call at 'Woodville', 176 Raddlebarn Road, at three o'clock Monday next, 10th June 1946?

This is our Mother and Baby Home and we shall have a baby boy for you.

He grinned.

You see?

The report from the Department of Health was highly satisfactory, it said. The Society were happy to go ahead as soon as arrangements could be made.

Violet shook her head. Would they bring him home straight away, just like that?

The letter didn't say.

She counted in her head. It was Thursday. They only had the weekend to prepare.

Violet, we're ready. Try to relax.

What about clothes, a cot? Violet asked.

For they were like people in a fable or rhyme, waiting for him to arrive, all wrapped up on their doorstep, like a prize.

40

My child, the nun called her, my child.

Violet sat with her hands folded in her lap. It was a bright, warm day. They must have taken the children out to play because there were some toys left scattered on the grass.

She looked at the clock. Ten past three. She would miss getting the boy up from his nap.

It was the third time she had been called in that month. The Mother Superior would ask pointedly how she was. Violet told her again that she needed a little more time, but that the boy was getting along fine.

Thriving, even.

The nun smoothed her habit down, straightened the wooden rosary beads around her neck.

Yes. The boy was growing up fast.

She paused, took a deep breath.

My child, she said. The older he is, the more attached he will become.

Violet stared out of the window behind her head. The nun cleared her throat, drew Violet's gaze back to meet her own.

She'd had a telephone call from Father McBride. There was a young couple. They were looking for a little boy.

Violet, she said. Might it be time?

41

They arrived ten minutes early, crunching up the gravel drive.

They walked up the stone steps and Fred rang the bell.

Father McBride would see them soon, the nun said. It was difficult to distinguish the shape of her features from the wimple fastened tight around her head.

They were shown into a reception room. Violet smoothed the pleat of her skirt before sitting down. Fred stood at the window looking out.

There were voices in the hallway, indistinct. Violet took a handkerchief from her bag, pressed it delicately to her chin.

There was a knock at the door and a younger nun came in. She couldn't have been more than Violet's age.

Pretty, Violet thought. Bit of a waste.

Sister Cathy was her name. She led them down the

hallway and stopped at a door, said they could ask her any questions that came to mind.

Sounds from the other side.

Fred had stepped back, the nun stood to his right.

He smiled as if willing Violet to move, go ahead. They had discussed it that morning, sitting up in bed. She should be the one to choose, he said.

But Father McBride had a boy in mind, she thought. Fred had taken her hand, squeezed it so that she looked him in the eyes.

But Vi. If it isn't right, it isn't right.

She'd nodded but felt the panic rise, shook her head.

How could she tell anything at first sight?

42

Violet had got up and gone to work like any normal day.

Bacon, eggs, two slices of white bread. Then Mass. Then various chores, then Father John had gone out.

He had eaten his lunch quickly, tiptoed about, even rinsed his own plate.

She was to wait there, Sister Cathy said. Someone would come and get her if the visit had gone well.

It was half past twelve, then two o'clock.

There were just a few shirts to be washed, some collars to be scrubbed.

Violet left them to soak, smoked a cigarette.

43

The door opened onto a quiet room, muted light. Sister Cathy went over to raise the blinds.

They nap from one until three, she said.

There were four iron cots in a row on her right.

In one of them, two babies slept at either end.

Are they twins? Violet asked.

The nun shook her head. Not by birth, but they'd arrived together and were inseparable, she said.

They continued along. Violet was trying to be discreet, not wanting to look. She couldn't think of any more questions to ask. The nun stood with her hands behind her back.

It was no good. She looked over her shoulder to find Fred.

As she turned, she saw, almost behind the door, an old pram. The hood was missing and the handle was crooked.

It was huge and deep like a boat. A child stood wobbling in it.

The nun nodded, gestured for her to proceed.

Violet smiled. The child mouthed sounds and squealed.

Violet beckoned for Fred to come in.

Look.

The child's head was a mess of golden curls.

This one, Violet said, is it a boy or a girl?

44

It was ten to four. Violet sat at the table with her jacket folded ready on her lap.

Perhaps no one was coming. Perhaps that was that.

Her bag was on the chair. She pulled out a large brown envelope. In it were cuttings, tokens, dockets. Deck A, Berth 4. Dining chits and a ticket for the train from York. Photographs, one of the nurses laughing on the ship. Letters on airmail paper, a translucent, pearlised shell. A banknote, a hymn sheet. A ribbon whose provenance she did not recall.

Violet looked at the fragments all spread out.

It was all she had to give him.

It was all she had of him to keep.

She scooped everything back in, put the envelope into her bag, walked to the dresser, folded a tea towel, came back.

She looked out of the window.

Sister Cathy was walking up the path.

45

Father McBride stood up, shook Fred's hand. Violet sat down.

He had all the papers here, he said.

Violet took the form he passed across. The child's name was written at the top.

Was it Welsh?

Yes.

I see.

Violet had the urge to say it out loud, wanted to feel the shape of it in her mouth. It was the name he would have been called for nine months. Every day, he would have heard its sounds, looked up in response.

She had never been to Wales.

The priest watched, seemed to understand.

Parents often change the name, he said, for one they have chosen themselves.

He leaned over and indicated the line below.

You may insert the new one here. In brackets, for now.

46

Violet followed Sister Cathy up the path. It felt for a moment like she might take her hand.

The Mother Superior was sitting at her desk.

The visit had gone well, she said.

She described the people they had found. A good Catholic couple, unable to have children of their own. Hard-working husband, respectable wife. Excellent report from the Department of Health.

The nun looked straight into her eyes, said again:

Violet. Don't you think it's time?

She slid a form across the desk. On one condition, Violet said, and picked up the pen.

I, the undersigned . . .

She wrote her name.

Being

(b) the mother of the infant

She crossed out all the other lines, ran her finger along the page.

Hereby state that I understand the nature of the adoption order for which this application is made. And that in particular I understand that the effect of the order will be

She closed her eyes, opened them again.

permanently to deprive me of my parental rights.

Violet ran her finger down the page to the last line. Then she shook her head back and signed.

47

Fred took Violet's hand in his.

The priest came back in. He was a little red in the face. He placed the file back on the desk.

May I ask your age, Mrs Hall?

Twenty-three.

Ah.

Violet blinked.

I'm afraid we cannot proceed after all.

Violet felt her throat constrict. Her cheeks were hot. Fred stood up.

The priest went stuttering on. Violet listened with her head tilted to one side. By law, he said, each spouse must be over twenty-five.

There was a pause.

I see, Violet said. Then what would you advise, Father?

Fred was stricken, his mouth was open but no words were coming out.

You could wait, the priest said. Or go ahead in the father's name alone.

Violet kept her hands folded in her lap.

The priest was saying what they already knew. There would be other babies, another boy, in a year or two.

Yes, Violet thought. There would be endless boys, for all time. She could almost feel them in the room, sticky-pawed, crowding round.

Fred sat down, seemed to slump almost. Violet cleared her throat, looked for him to speak. The priest shuffled the forms, offered apologies for the mistake.

Then Violet felt it spread like a rash across her face; in the muscles of her jaw tightening, in her spine straightening.

How foolish she had been. Now finally it came.

Shame.

Shame that he was not her own.

So many times she had planned how to explain it to everyone else. How she would say, casually but with pride, that he had been raised a Catholic from the start. That he came from a good home. That the mother, poor girl, had done the best by him she could.

After all, she would say, it happened a lot.

And she had sewn and patched and saved every last scrap of herself for him. Darning, stitching, mending everything against its will, trying to fill everything back up. Ready for who? A boy born to someone else then handed down, nearly new.

Would she ever be enough?

Violet looked up. The priest was busying himself with the papers on his desk.

She turned to Fred. He met her eyes with an expression she hadn't seen before. Perhaps, she thought, it was something she hadn't seen back then, after he carried her down the stairs in the dark, her sopping nightdress sticking to her skin.

He looked distraught, defeated, like he might finally give in.

No.

There was only this one. This boy, bouncing in the pram.

Violet shook her head.

It doesn't matter, she said.

The boy was meant for them.

48

Violet waited in the nun's office alone. She thought of the boy, imagined him there with her now, straining to get down out of her lap, hands grabbing at the desk, knocking over the pencil pot; the letter opener spinning to a stop and pencil shavings spilled, sticking like frills to his fingers and toes.

Down the hall, at the front of the house, Violet knew how it would go. Papers taken in and out of envelopes; hands shaken, shaken again; another signature, a donation gratefully received; a drawer unlocked, opened and shut.

Yet nothing else had changed. The statue of the Virgin Mary still stood beside the desk. And the painting of Saul kneeling in the dust, his horse rearing up.

It was then that Violet felt the crushing weight, and bowed her head.

She waited for a sign.

No. There was nothing left to say.

For the Lord giveth, and the Lord taketh away.

49

The papers were gathered up, copies torn off.

Adoption Order in Respect of an Infant.

Fred had crossed out every 'We' and written 'I' instead.

The priest added a note to the side.

Wife to make application when she is twenty-five.

Father McBride looked flushed.

There is one more thing, Mrs Hall.

Violet caught her breath.

The natural mother of the child, she has asked to meet you, the mother, before . . .

He trailed off, started again.

In order to be reassured, you see? It's rather unconventional, but we feel on this occasion, given that the boy has been with us for quite a while . . .

Violet let her shoulders drop, nodded, relieved. The priest too breathed out, pulled his handkerchief from his pocket and wiped his brow.

Then I am delighted to say that you may take him home with you today.

Fred stood up, loosened his limbs.

Thank you, Father.

He leaned over to shake his hand.

Violet coughed. One more thing, Father, may I ask?

The priest looked askance, wary again.

The boy's mother. Am I permitted to know her name?

50

The cots stood vacant and the old pram in the corner was still. All was order, all was clean.

She sat with you on the rug. She pulled you up by your hands, you wobbled, stood. You looked away, wanting her to hide her face.

Peepo!

Gone.

You held out your arms to be picked up.

You put your head on her shoulder. You put your thumb in your mouth.

Remember?

Cast your mind back, beyond the prefabricated shack of what you know. Long ago, it was. Blank slate you were, mind-slow. Aglow instead with light and moving shapes, bathed in the rose-tint of afternoon stone, sweat smells and talc, fig-split, your Mama's mouth and cherries, pips spat out. Remember in the chapel where she held you out? And the Virgin Mary looked down with a smile that it was difficult to place, as the water trickled over your face.

Then you were carried, home. Tipped out on the tarmac like a stone, hardened off in the crisp cold of the cabbage patch.

And then the search began. How you searched, found little; searched again, found more. All those letters to institutions domestic and overseas, searching like a boy-cub blindly nosing for its mother's teat. Searching in secret, there a sign, there a trace. A stamp, a form, a phrase, a crossing-out.

And you found that you were carried there and back. Birthed and spit-dabbed, suckled, warmed and cooled. Calmed through colic, blessed, baptised, clasped tight or yielded, wrapped.

Yes.

Clapped and giddied, little piggied all the way home. Smiled at, howling, powder-puffed. Held aloft, stroked and kissed, oh! Pram Boy, kissed at corner and crease; brushed lightly against her cheek.

And when you grew up and found her, she knew. When she saw you for the first time, standing on her doorstep, her first thought was that you bore some resemblance to her eldest son. The one she had after you.

And there, you began; sat for cups of tea, asked questions; told her things you had learned that she did not know.

You sent her files to check and checked your facts.

It took her back.

Looking at you, she remembered him. His delicate hands, the sewing machine. His head bent forward, hair parted on the side. She remembered how she held her breath their first time, down in the furrows of the wooded earth. And then, later, alone, the pill-throw.

She gave you cuttings crumpled, papers stamped, dockets clocked to deck and berth. A single, bright blond curl.

For her, she kept the memory of being at bow and stern, and the slow light of the Mediterranean coming round. And the heft of her pregnant body moving through the sounds and stench, and finally, her sun-stroked shoulders and the burn, the dazzling beauty of the water they were in. The downy softness of her lover's skin.

All along she knew you, while you knew her not.

And she was game, when you took your teenage daughters out to meet her and they played at guessing whose was what (a stubborn streak, her cheekbones, curls, her height). And she held her hand out palm to palm, laughed, took off her shoes, compared her feet.

Yes. She remembered that the light was warm and low that day. The cots stood vacant; the pram was still.

She remembered the slow blink of your eyes and the gentle motion of your mouth.

You put your hand to her face. You spread your fingers against her cheek, resettled yourself on her hip.

She remembered the weight and warmth of your head on her shoulder.

She remembered the open palm of your hand.

She remembered your fingers, she remembered your face.

She whispered into your ear.

And she kissed your face.

And she kissed your face and said (knowing that the woman she had met would take her place):

Yes.

I
will
see
you
again

my
son.

51

Before your mother died, she thought that he was there and calling her to come, your father; flung back her arm to feel the empty cool of his side of the bed, dreamt of him, knew he was there, she said.

And knew what age the twins would then have been. And recalled the pail of thin red blood.

She had been carried, she said, as if through a flood.

Then waiting for him to come home from the war, then starting over again.

And your curls. And your bowed legs that she attributed not to rickets as was likely, but the way you bounced in the bottomless pram with its deep curved bed.

And she told the joke about the playpen and the cot and the story, a little later on, about the baby girl they brought home next. Except you saw her off; she did not take. And anyway, she said, my nerves were frayed.

Before your mother died, you showed her what you had gleaned from years of research. An archive of the circumstances of your birth. And she added to your files all that she had: black-and-white and pink and green the forms, the letter-headed papers, gothic font. You saw their applications for consent, the margins full of pencil-scrawls and notes:

Child born in Italy
Army Cert produced
Wife to make application when she is twenty-five.

And yet, when your mother died she had outlived them all, waiting until last to claim her time. She missed the feel of the piano keys and yes, envied the ease of others' lives. She knew what age the twins would then have been, recalled the blood, the pail, the joke about the playpen and the cot; recalled which child was born to whom, outside of wedlock.

But Pram Boy, do you know why, when your mother died, she waited until you left her hospital bed?

No goodbye, that way, not again.

For your mothers did not leave you; you were kept.

Acknowledgements

Thank you to my father for trusting me to make something wildly imagined and new. And to my whole family. Thank you to Emma Paterson for seeing something there and calling it a novel, to Monica MacSwan and Max Porter. Thanks to all at Granta, in particular Anne Meadows, Rowan Cope, Jason Arthur, Jenny Page, Christine Lo, Patty Rennie and Lamorna Elmer. Thanks to friends who have advised, encouraged and inspired: Helen Ward and Oli Evans, Leslie Hill and Helen Paris, Miranda Collinge, Vic Kitchingman, Georgia Rutherford. Special thanks to Jo Kociejowski and Liz Timperley-Preece for reading with honesty and openness. Thanks also and as ever to Katie Natanel for reading, listening and sharing with acuity and insight. Thank you to Margot, Stanley, Gloria and Ruth, who are all here. And to Matthew, always and for everything and for notes on every draft. Thank you to both our mothers for their encouragement and support. Finally, thank you to Eileen and Eileen for bold lives lived.